Nashville Trio

A Music City Mènage

Cover design by Randall Luttenberg
Interior Design by BookSculpting
Edited by Polish Editing

Ebook ISBN: 9-781-9408-8603-9
Print ISBN: 978-1-940886-04-6

Manufactured in the United States of America
First Edition May 2014

The author acknowledges the copyrighted or trademarked status and trademark owners of the following wordmarks mentioned in this work of fiction: Harley Fat Boy.

Nashville Trio

A MUSIC CITY MÈNAGE

Joy Daniels

Other books by Joy Daniels

FICTION:

HIDE AND SEEK

REVVING HER UP (FULL THROTTLE #1)

LIGHTS OUT (IN: WE LOVE NEW YORK)

UNMASKED (IN: REVEALED, ENTWINED VOL. 2)

NON-FICTION:

SEX TELLS THE STORY (IN: FIFTY WRITERS ON FIFTY SHADES OF GREY)

Chapter One

The last guitar notes faded into the bar's stuffy air, and Ashley Ford looked down, avoiding everyone's eyes. The session had sucked for the second day in a row, and everyone knew why. Knew who was to blame. She stared at the guitar in her hands, running her fingers down the long neck, and strummed a few chords. The instrument still worked fine – she was the one who was out of tune.

She'd come in late on "Cruel-hearted Man", sounded half-asleep on "Cherry Pie," and stumbled over the lyrics to "Baby Been Gone Too Long" – songs she'd written, and could sing in her sleep. *What the hell was going on?*

A stool scraped across the floor nearby, and Rob Porter, her best friend and housemate, and the other half of the duo Sweet Talk, stood up, and looked around the room. "That's it for today, folks. We'll wrap it up now, and see y'all at Bootleggers Sunday night."

Heads bobbed, and a murmur of interest swept the room. Instead of playing in their usual Nashville bar, Sweet Talk was opening for We Were Angels, a hot country act that was climbing the charts. It was a great opportunity, the kind that could introduce Sweet Talk to hundreds of potential fans, and maybe even a new recording contract.

If she didn't screw it up.

The backup players hopped off their stools, stretched, and started to scatter. Out of the corner of her eye, Ashley caught Rob casting a smoldering look across the room. She followed his gaze to the bass player they'd borrowed for the show. He was Rob's type – sexy, male, and available. An emotion she couldn't – *wouldn't* – name prodded her in the gut, and she looked away.

A hand landed on her shoulder. She leaned towards it instinctively, and Rob's arm wrapped around her, his hand resting on her bicep. Pleasure skittered across her skin from the points of contact and she shivered. His denim-clad leg brushed against her arm, and her nipples tingled.

What the hell? Ashley pulled away, and rubbed the knot forming between her eyes. She and Rob had always had great creative chemistry, but this was different. It was *physical*.

Rob turned to her. His brow furrowed with concern, and she attempted a smile. It must have come out like a grimace because his expression darkened. He tilted his head in question.

Please don't ask me what's wrong. I'm running out of excuses. She sure as hell couldn't tell him the truth – that in addition to her downward-spiraling career, her sudden attraction to her gay best friend and co-singer was morphing into a full-blown obsession.

She attempted another smile. It must have looked better this time because he smiled back. "So what will it be, Ash? Fried chicken from the Musicman Grill or mac n' cheese from Mama's Kitchen?"

Southern comfort food. He was trying to cheer her up. She shook her head. "Nothing for me. I'm not really hungry."

Rob's eyes narrowed, and Ashley prayed that none of her inner turmoil showed on her face. She put her guitar on the stand. "I need to run some errands. Pick up some new strings before Abe's Music closes."

Rob squatted down in front of her bringing them to eye level. She started to look away but he grasped her chin with two gentle fingers, and turned it towards him. Her gaze fastened on his mouth, and her heart thumped painfully in her chest. A few inches forward and she could kiss him.

How would his lips feel? Warm and soft? Firm and hot? And if she slipped her tongue between them... She closed her eyes to remove the temptation.

"It's okay, Ash. We'll do better next week."

She shook her head with a bitter laugh. "We, Rob? *We're* not wasting everyone's time by playing like crap."

Rob gently shook her chin, and she opened her eyes. Although he'd been nothing but supportive over these past few months, Ashley dreaded the day she'd see disappointment in his warm brown gaze. He gave her a sympathetic smile. "Don't be so hard on yourself, Ash. Everyone goes through bad patches. We'll get through this. Now come on, let's get something to eat."

Rob stood, and pulled her to her feet, then slung an arm over her shoulder. Desire rocketed through her, and her mouth went dry. She gritted her teeth but couldn't hold back the delicious shiver that skittered over her skin. Thankfully, he didn't seem to notice.

Rob guided them through the maze of equipment towards the door. It opened before they reached it, and a man stepped in, silhouetted in the late afternoon light. Rob raised a hand in greeting to their personal manager, Brad Hamilton. They hadn't arranged to meet today but Ashley wasn't surprised to see him – Brad seemed to spend most of his waking hours circulating among the recording companies, studios, and clubs that filled Nashville's Music Row.

They reached Brad's side, and he held the door open. "I saw some of your players heading down the street. How'd the practice go?"

Ashley stepped through to the sidewalk and squinted in the sudden brightness. She didn't hear Rob's reply but when Brad answered, "That's great," she knew he'd lied for her. Again.

"Off to lunch?" Brad asked.

"I'm heading over to the Musicman Grill to join some of the guys. Ashley has some errands to run." The look Rob gave her said that he knew it was an excuse. She shrugged.

Brad nodded. "If you've got a minute, I wanted to run some ideas past you." He put a hand on Ashley's arm. "It's nothing that important, so no need to interrupt your errands."

Rob shook his head. "Can it wait? If you have some ideas for us, I want Ash there when we discuss them."

A strange expression crossed Brad's face, and Ashley got the weird feeling that he'd been trying to get rid of her. To talk to Rob alone.

Why would Brad want to do that? Was he keeping something from her?

She shook her head. She was imagining things, her current funk making her see threats where there were none. She opened her mouth to speak when she caught sight of something over Brad's shoulder. Something that made the breath freeze in her chest.

Sunlight glinting off silver-gray metal. Yellow trim. Curved handlebars. Her heart revved, and her mouth went dry.

Gooseflesh rose on her arms. *It couldn't be...*

The two men turned to follow her gaze, and Rob let out a low whistle. "Nice bike. Haven't seen one of those babies in years."

Brad nodded. "Classic Harley Fat Boy. Seen it there a couple of times." Brad pointed to the marquee. "Must belong to one of the head honchos of the new club."

Rob and Brad launched into a discussion of The Roadhouse, the club that was set to open soon across the street. She tried to tune into what was being said, but couldn't tear her attention away from the bike. *Bug-eyed headlight. Leather seat.* Muscles clenched deep in her core, and her nipples tightened into peaks. She crossed her arms to hide her sudden arousal.

There was a pause in the men's conversation, and from the corner of her eye Ashley could see Rob looking at her, his gaze going from her to the bike and back. "Something wrong Ash?

She shook her head. "Nothing. That bike looked familiar. Reminded me of someone." *Someone I left behind years ago.*

"A lucky someone if he owns a bike like that," Brad said with an appreciative smile.

The men nodded in agreement. Brad jerked a thumb towards the club. "I got to run. Gonna talk to those honchos, and convince them that Sweet Talk would be perfect for their opening night."

She gave Brad a weak smile. The Roadhouse's grand opening was all Nashville was talking about these days, and being part of it would be a career-making opportunity for Sweet Talk – if she could figure out what the hell was wrong with her, and make it right before then.

After promising to let them know how it went, Brad shook Rob's hand, gave Ashley a quick peck on the cheek, and took off.

Rob turned to her. "Are you sure you don't want company? We could find a café somewhere, just you and me, and talk."

Right, like she needed more *time alone with Rob.* Ashley shook her head. "I need a little space. Time to think."

"Don't think too much." He held up a hand before she could protest. "You know what I mean. You overthink everything. Sometimes you got to go with your gut, Ash. Think with your heart, not your head."

Ashley cocked her head, and furrowed her brow in mock confusion. "Wait, do you want me to go with my heart," she pointed to her chest, "or my gut?" She laid a hand over her middle.

Rob shook his head with a laugh. "You know what I mean, smartass." His expression turned serious again, and he tapped her on the forehead. "Not all the answers are in here. You have to trust yourself. We'll get through whatever is bothering you. You'll see."

All she saw was her musical future slipping away, but she smiled for Rob's sake. He held out his arms, and Ashley stepped into them. For a moment she indulged in the feel of those strong biceps around her shoulders, that rock hard chest against her cheek. He stroked her hair, and shivers of contentment danced down her spine. With a mental groan she stepped back before she could get too comfortable. Or aroused.

She needed to put some distance between them. Real distance. But where could she go? She knew she was always welcome at Granny's, but was the situation with Rob bad enough to warrant a return to the town she'd fled three years ago?

Rob pursed his lips in thought, making him look like he was puckering up for a kiss. Ashley's breasts tightened. Yes. It was time to retreat, and, Oak Valley was the logical place to go.

He opened his mouth, but his stomach jumped in with a low growl. The sound broke through the misery that had gripped Ashley all day, and she smiled. She pointed at him with a laugh. "Sounds like you should go with your gut – to lunch. I'll be okay. Really."

He planted a kiss on her forehead. "Okay, babe. I'll see you in a bit."

She watched him turn and lope across the street, then forced her attention away from his jeans-clad ass. With a last glance at glittering chrome and leather, she turned on her heel, leaving both man and motorcycle behind.

Chapter Two

Ashley sat up in her bed, ears straining to pick up a sound. There it was again: the soft shuffle of someone moving across the carpet. Next came a bump, then a mumbled curse. Rob was home. Another bump and a low chuckle followed by humming. Ashley could make out a few bars of the song they'd played around with at practice earlier in the day. She glanced at the clock. For Rob to come in humming and laughing at three a.m. meant only one thing.

He'd gotten lucky.

Jealousy and lust prodded her, as they always did when she thought of Rob with a man. He'd been hooking up a lot lately so the confusing feelings had become familiar. Who had he gone for this time? He seemed to prefer lanky brunettes. An image flashed into her mind of her singing partner with a sexy, dark-haired man. Rob's guitar-calloused fingers buried in black hair, his buff body pressed up against another man's...

Ashley's core tightened, and she turned on her side, trying to will the arousing thoughts away. She was *not* going to think about her roommate like this anymore. They were friends for God's sake.

The shuffling and humming paused outside her door. When the soft footsteps turned towards the bathroom Ashley let out the breath she'd been holding. The soft clang of a belt buckle hitting the bathmat was followed by the sound of the shower turning on. *All those beautiful muscles naked in the shower just steps from her door.* Water drowned out the rest of Rob's movements, but his satisfied groan filtered into her room.

Was that what he sounded like when he came?

Her thighs tensed. As if independent from her body, her hand crept up to cup one breast. With thumb and forefinger she pinched the stiff nipple, and bit her lip to hold back a moan. Her other hand skimmed down her torso, and slipped beneath her pajama bottoms. She felt guilty using her roommate like this, but fantasizing about Rob and his conquests was the only way to release the awful tension that gripped her these days. What he didn't know couldn't hurt him, right?

She retrieved a vibrator from the drawer of her nightstand. Although she preferred a stronger buzz she turned it to the lowest setting – less chance that Rob would hear it when the water stopped. In the weeks since Rob had started trolling bars she'd gotten it down perfectly. She could bring herself to orgasm in the time that it took him to shower and rub himself down.

Mmm, rub down. Two male bodies. Slippery and wet. Deep muscles clenched in her womb. With one hand kneading her breast, she brought the smooth vibrating head under her pajama bottoms, and between her lower lips. The shaft touched her clit, and her whole body jerked. She circled her swollen bud with the wand, and sparks shot from her womb up her spine. She conjured an image of Rob with a sexy, dark-haired stranger. Arms entangled. Cocks hard and ready. She stroked the vibrator from her clit to her wet opening and back. Slowly at first, then faster, encouraging that delicious pressure to build. Vibrations danced through her pussy as naked men wrestled in her head.

The water stopped. Rob was stepping out of the shower now. *Naked, dripping*. She moved the vibrator faster, and pinched her other nipple, rolling it between her fingers. Her head tossed against the pillow, and she fought to keep silent. He'd hear her now that the shower was off. The bathroom door opened. *Just a little more*. It was taking her longer than usual. She focused on the image in her head and pressed her hips up to meet the toy. Her inner muscles spasmed. *Almost there...*

Another face popped into her mind alongside Rob's – one with dark hair and blue eyes like a frozen lake on a clear day. A tall lean body, known to straddle a classic Harley Fat boy.

Her beautiful ex, Ty Monroe.

Her clit began to twitch, she was so close, but she shook her head. She would not let *that* man intrude on her fantasy. She tried to recall the generic brunette she'd pictured earlier but he had been replaced by the all-too-familiar face and body of her ex, entwined with Rob.

Three years and two hundred miles between them, and that damned man was still interfering with her life. She tried again to force him from her mind, but met with little success. The more she tried, the harder it got. The hotter *she* got. It was the sexiest thing she had ever imagined.

Rob and Ty...

With a snort of disgust she turned the vibrator off, and shoved it aside. It fell to the floor with a clunk. Footsteps paused outside her door. "Ash? You up?"

She froze, her body strung tight from her near-orgasm. She could ignore Rob, but he'd probably poke his head in anyway. She yanked her hand away from her breast, and tugged her shirt down. "I'm up." She snatched a tissue from her bedside table to clean the musky evidence of her pleasure off her fingers.

The door opened to reveal Rob's muscular body backlit by the hall light. Ashley's gaze roamed over his perfect form. Messy blond hair brushed his broad shoulders and chest. Her gaze continued down to a narrow waist, and strong solid legs. Even more beautiful in the flesh than in her fantasy. Her pussy muscles quivered.

"I woke you up, didn't I? Sorry." Rob shifted, crossing his arms, and leaning against the doorjamb. Her throat went dry. The light fell on his chest, and her eyes were drawn down the damp line of hair trailing into the towel he'd tucked around his hips. In the three years they'd lived together she'd caught him naked a few times, and knew a serious prize hid beneath that towel. Not for the first time she wondered: did he take it in the ass or did other men feel that stallion cock in theirs? Again she imagined Rob with Ty, and her clit tingled. She clenched her thighs together, and forced herself to look up at his face.

"Come in." Her voice came out low and husky. *I hope he thinks it's because I just woke up, not because I'm fantasizing about him fucking a hot guy*. She cleared her throat. "I was having a strange dream anyway."

Rob sauntered around the far side of the bed, and flung himself down beside her. The towel somehow managed to stay in place. *Bummer*.

"What was it about?"

She shrugged, unable to follow the lie with anything convincing. "Nothing important. I just remember that I didn't like it." That was almost the truth – imagining Ty with Rob had been hot, but disturbing too.

Rob propped himself up on one elbow, resting his head in

his hand. The other hand reached up to brush her hair from her eyes. She probably looked terrible, her red hair a rat's nest of frizz and curls. Good thing their relationship was platonic.

Yeah, good thing.

"Poor Ash."

Frustration was bad enough – the last thing she wanted was pity. She changed the subject. "So, how was the party?"

"Good. *Really* good."

She nodded, not surprised. She knew she shouldn't ask, shouldn't torture herself, but she couldn't resist. "So who was the lucky boy tonight?" She managed to keep the eagerness out of her voice.

Rob chuckled, a low sound that made her every nerve stretch taut like a guitar string. "Oh, he was a hot one, Ash. Tall with blue eyes and dark hair."

A brunette. Score one for Ashley. She tried to keep a certain dark-haired blue-eyed man from her mind, and failed. Again.

Rob continued. "Muscular but not too built – you know the type I like."

Ashley tried to fight the jealousy rising in her gut. "You gonna see him again?"

"Nah. He was from out of town. But man, was he pretty, with pale blue eyes that looked like..." Rob shook his head. "I can't describe them."

She tried to sound nonchalant. "Like a frozen lake on a clear day?"

Rob turned to look at her. "Exactly!" He ruffled her hair with a smile. "That's why you're the wordsmith in our duo. But how did you know?

She shrugged. "I knew a guy with eyes like that."

"Who?"

She heard the concern in his voice and forced herself to sound casual. "No one you know. Just some guy from back home."

"Speaking of home, tell me why you're leaving me again?" Rob tried to lighten his tone but it still came out as a growl.

"I'm not leaving you – I'm going home to visit Granny. It has been three years since I've been back." She thumped him on the chest. "You're the one who's always telling me to take a break."

That made sense. So why did he get the feeling something else was going on? Was she trying to get away from *him*? Their relationship was intense - working and living together - but he tried not to crowd her. To give her the space she seemed to need. "Of course I want you to see your Granny. But I get the feeling you're not just running *towards* something, know what I mean?"

A guilty sort of look darkened her green eyes, but it disappeared before Rob could be sure.

"I'm not running away. I just need a break. You know, to get away from the Nashville scene. The fishbowl," she made air quotes around the word, "as you call it."

She needed a break, and he was officially being a jerk about it. He shook his head to get rid of his suspicions, and forced a smile. "Then I'm glad you're going – but don't forget we have a show on Sunday."

"As if I would. I'll be back in plenty of time. Maybe I'll drag Val along to see us."

Rob nodded. Never hurt to have a familiar face in the audience. "Anyone else you're looking forward to seeing back home? Old friends?"

Ashley's hands stilled against the sheets. "Not really."

He took a breath and tried to sound casual. "How about that ex of yours, Ty?"

She shrugged. "I'm sure he left town years ago."

And if he hadn't? How would she react if she ran into the man who had broken her heart, and almost derailed her dreams – and Rob's? He took a breath. "What are you going to do if he's still there? If you run into him in the grocery store or diner?"

Ashley's eyes went wide for a moment, and she shook her head. "Nothing – because it ain't gonna happen. Why?"

"I'm worried about you, Ash. Wouldn't want to see you blindsided on top of everything else you're dealing with."

A shadow passed over Ashley's face. Rob could have kicked himself for bringing up her troubles. He sat up, and wrapped an arm around her shoulders. She smelled like shampoo mingled with his spicy soap. An image of Ashley wearing lather and nothing else flashed through his mind. His balls tightened, and his cock twitched under the towel.

Whoa, where the hell had that come from? Rob had realized long ago that those feelings had no place in their relationship. He was usually better about reining them in. He shook his head to clear it, and pulled back, putting some distance between them. "So, he's not the reason you haven't been back?"

She dismissed the idea with a wave. "No, end of story. So tell me more about your boy toy tonight."

Rob snorted at her attempt to change the subject. "You are far too interested in my escapades. How long has it been since *you've* had sex?" He leaned against the pillow, trying to act as if he wasn't really, *really* interested in her answer.

She punched playfully him on the bicep. "Rob! That's none

of your business."

Her reaction was ridiculous since she was forever asking about his sex life, but he let that go. "Honey, I'm your housemate, co-singer, and business partner. *Everything* you do is my business. Besides unless you've gotten really crafty and sly, I can answer that question myself: three years." He looked her in the eye. "It has been three years right? I mean you were getting some from Ty weren't you? Before I took you away for all this." His arm swept the room.

"For what – the curtains?"

Rob laughed, and elbowed her in the ribs. "No, the Nashville dream, baby. It's going to be ours soon. I can taste it." He put up a hand when she started shaking her head. "I know what you're thinking, Ash, and you're wrong. Every artist goes through down periods. You'll pull out of this and be better than ever."

She didn't look convinced.

He rolled onto his side so they were face-to-face. "I knew you had what it took to make it in Nashville the moment I heard you sing, Ash. That hasn't changed."

He'd met her at a county fair, on the last leg of a summer tour he'd done with his former band. Their back-up singer had split a couple of stops earlier, and Rob was on the verge of calling it quits himself when they reached the Seventy-fifth Annual Warrington County Fair. He'd heard plenty of mediocre performers at these events, so when "Oak Valley's own Ashley Ford" was announced as an opening act he hadn't expected much. Then she'd started singing.

He smiled. "Do you know what attracted me to you that night, Ash? Why I asked you to join me onstage?"

She shook her head.

"Your energy. Your *fire*." He'd also fallen for her gorgeous red curls, green eyes, and lush hot body, but he kept that to himself. "When we sang together there was such chemistry between us. *Passion*. Didn't you feel it?"

She nodded slowly. Rob grabbed her shoulder. "You just need to tap into that passion again, Ash."

She tilted her head, and looked at him as if trying to figure something out. A panicked feeling gripped Rob's gut. Had he given too much away? Time to change the subject.

He sat up, pointing at her. "Maybe that's your problem – you need to get laid. Have a few escapades of your own. Sex can be very stimulating to your creativity," he added when she started to shake her head.

She frowned. "Hook up with a stranger in a bar, like you do? Yeah, that would do wonders for my muse."

Without stopping to think, he leaned down, and nuzzled her neck. "You wouldn't have to go to a bar. I'd be happy to help."

She pushed him away. "Yeah right, Rob. You like boys remember? If you haven't noticed, I'm not a boy."

"Sugar," he said, laying on the Texas drawl, "I *know* you're not a boy. I've seen you naked, and you got all sorts of nice bits that I don't have. Bits I wouldn't mind seeing a bit closer..." He tugged on the edge of the cover, pretending to it pull it down.

What would happen if she let him pull the covers away? If she let him explore that beautiful body, plumb the depths between her thighs–?

What the hell was he doing? He let go of the blanket like it had caught on fire, and flopped back onto the bed. Ashley yanked the covers to her chin. He cleared his throat. "As I've told you before, I'm not gay, I'm bi."

She rolled her eyes. "So you say – but if that's true why don't you ever pick-up women?"

Why didn't he? It was a question he'd asked himself a lot recently, but had yet to answer. "It's complicated."

Ashley lay down next to him. "Whatever."

He shifted to hide the erection that poked against his towel. After years of picking up men in bars, he had propositioned his best friend – and been turned down.

It didn't get any more complicated than that.

Chapter Three

An ear-piercing shriek rent the air. Ashley's hair stood on end, and she grabbed Granny's porch railing to keep from tumbling down the steps. A woman in a chest-hugging tee shirt waved from the window of the pick-up truck that had pulled up in front of Granny's house. Ashley had been in town for less than two hours, but it was long enough for Val Coleman to track her down.

Val jumped out of the truck, flung her hands up to her cheeks, and opened her mouth wide. Ashley laughed. Val had perfected her "fan-girl face" years ago, practicing it in the mirror alongside Ashley's Country Music Entertainer of the Year Award acceptance speech. Ashley braced herself but still winced as another cry sounded at closer range. She'd never understood how the Beatles had survived such shrieks without going deaf.

Val bounded up the steps, and grabbed Ashley's hands. "Oh my God! If it isn't the famous Nashville singing sensation, Ashley Ford! Oh please, Miss Ford, can I have your autograph – and a picture of Rob Porter naked in the shower?"

Ashley laughed. Rob had a fabulous voice and magic fingers on the guitar, but there was no doubt that his looks were as big a draw as his talent with the women in their audience – and a good portion of the men too. "Taking pictures of Rob will only pump up his ego even more and trust me; it's substantial enough as it is."

"I bet that's not all that's substantial on that boy. Come on, can't you share a little with your oldest friend? I just want to know – is he really as well hung as he looks in those tight black jeans? Because I've tried to guess and–"

Ashley held up a hand. She'd come home to get away from fantasizing about what hung behind Rob's fly – she didn't need Val to get her started again. "Val, I am not discussing my partner's endowments with you."

Val laughed. "You know I'm just riling you up, girl. You can keep your secrets." She gave Ashley a wink. "I'll have to find out in some other way." Val looped her arm through Ashley's, and pulled her towards Granny's porch swing. As soon as they were settled, she took Ashley's hands. "So what brings you back, babe? Not that I'm not happy to see you but after three years of trying to get your butt back here for a visit, I know you didn't come for a glass of Mrs. Ida's sweet tea."

Ashley opened her mouth to dismiss Val's concern but stopped. This was Val – the friend who had stuck with her through everything, in spite of the fact that Ashley had been AWOL from Oak Valley for so long. Thankfully, Val was too good-hearted to hold a grudge, and had come to Nashville a few times to see Sweet Talk perform.

Ashley took a deep breath. "I needed a break, you know? My last performance... well, it wasn't too hot. And our latest practice session sucked. I feel off. Flat. Like the fire's gone out." She took a deep breath. "I'm afraid I've lost it."

Val shook her head sympathetically but there was a

hard gleam in her eye. "You know that's nonsense. You were born with talent, girl – it's not something you can lose." Her expression softened. "Maybe you just need a break. Some rest and relaxation back among your people."

Ashley snorted. "I only lived in Oak Valley for ten years – that makes me a newcomer in the eyes of most people around here." Ashley was surprised to hear a note of bitterness in her words. After so long, could she still feel wounded by the rejection of the townspeople in the only place she had ever lived long enough to call home?

Val brushed her words aside. "Please. Everyone in this town follows you as closely as they do the high school football team. They've claimed you, girl. You're a local whether you want to be or not." She pushed a toe against the ground, setting the swing rocking. "So, how long are you in town?"

"A couple of days. We're opening for We Were Angels in one of the better Nashville clubs on Sunday night, so I gotta head back that morning."

Val nodded. "Okay, so we got a day and a half for some serious R & R. I can work with that."

Ashley smiled. Of course, Val would take it as a challenge – and come up with a plan. Sure enough, the other woman nodded. "I'm having some folks over for a barbecue tomorrow. The usual crowd mostly, but a couple of new faces. Bring your bathing suit. The lake is still too cold but the pool is great."

Ashley nodded. She'd heard a few years back that Val had purchased one of the vacation houses by the lake, and turned it into a year-round residence.

Val continued. "Tonight we'll head down to Charley's. Bring your guitar. I know everyone would enjoy a few songs from our very own homegrown star."

Ashley held up a hand. "No, no—." She stopped mid-protest. *Why not?* Maybe that was what she needed to get out of her slump. Not to get laid, as Rob suggested, but to get back to her roots. Play a few songs for the hometown crowd. No Nashville spotlight, no record execs to impress, no pressure.

Val took her hesitation for refusal. "Come on, it will be fun. Remember what a blast we had going to hole-in-the-wall bars all over the county so you could play?"

Ashley nodded. From the time Ashley had gotten her first guitar at ten years old, she'd wanted to be a country music singer. As soon as Val had gotten her driver's license – a full six months earlier than Ashley – they'd driven to every town within a hundred miles to find places where Ashley could perform. And no matter how rundown the bar or small the crowd, she'd loved every minute of it.

She laughed. "Do you think anyone was convinced by the terrible fake IDs we used to get into those places?"

Val shook her head. "We weren't using the IDs to buy alcohol, so they were willing to pretend. They just wanted to hear you play."

Ashley smiled. "Okay Val. I'll do it."

Ty felt the voice before he heard it. Sultry, smooth tones that slid down his spine and across his belly, leaving heat in their wake. The next verse headed further south, tightening his balls, and sending jolts of electricity across his skin when he realized whom it belonged to. Only one woman sang like that. Only one woman had the power to tune him in and turn him on from across the room.

Ashley Ford was back in town. Ty frowned. It sounded like the title of a damned country song.

He stood in the in the shadows at the back of the room, and allowed himself a single moment of indulgence. Closing his eyes, he let her voice wash over him, reaching for that soul-deep place he'd sealed off three years ago...

He shook his head. Not going there. Not this time. He forced his eyes open, and focused straight ahead. He skirted the tables that stood in his way, and came up beside the bar, only then allowing himself to face the woman on the stage. To stare.

He wasn't the only one. Every eye was fixed on the petite redhead perched on the barstool. She'd been a regular fixture at Charley's once, but that was before.

She wore a black leather vest laced up over a white V-neck, revealing a pale slice of cleavage between full breasts. Faded jeans clung to ripe curves, and disappeared into a pair of black high-heeled boots straight out of an S & M fantasy. Long red curls cascaded over her shoulders, and his fingers curled around the memory of those silken strands. Her eyes were closed, her head thrown back. She caressed the strings of her instrument like a lover, and when her hand slid up the guitar's neck, Ty's cock swelled against his fly.

Damn. He exhaled deeply to will his arousal down. To think of all the times he'd been in Nashville over the past year, wondering if he'd run into her... He shook his head.

The song ended. There were a few scattered claps, but most people seemed too stunned to applaud. They sat in silence, waiting, and she didn't disappoint. Humming along with the first few notes, she began a quiet song. He recognized the lyrics to "An Honest Woman." She'd been working on it when that damned singer swept her out of town.

The last notes died out, and the crowd held its collective breath. Ty found that he was holding his as well, and exhaled with a soft curse. She strummed a few chords, then launched into an upbeat song. Every toe was tapping, and every face smiling, before the chorus. She grinned. She couldn't possibly see anyone beyond the floodlight shining into her face, but that wouldn't stop each person from feeling as if she smiled just for them.

He knew how they felt. He'd felt that magic up close and personal. For one incredible year she'd been his. And then she was gone.

Chapter Four

Ashley finished the song, letting the last notes fade before she looked up. The crowd showed its appreciation with applause, and catcalls. She smiled, waving in the direction of where she thought Val had been sitting, and the stage light flicked off.

She rolled her shoulders, and placed her guitar against the wall. From the corner of her eye she saw some familiar faces approaching the stage. She smiled, and pointed to the back hallway. Let them think she needed the bathroom. She wasn't ready to talk to anyone yet.

Shaking her head, she tried to free the hairs that stuck to her forehead and the back of her neck. She couldn't blame the one light pointed at the stage, so it had to be nerves that were making her hands damp and her brow shine. She stepped around the amp and made her way over the tangle of cords that snaked their way to the outlet. The stage was low enough that she could hop off the front, but she preferred the steps half-hidden in the shadows.

She made her way to the ladies', and stared at herself in the mirror. She frowned. Had anyone noticed that she'd started off flat? Or that her timing was off at the beginning of "An Honest

Woman"? She shook her head. She'd hoped that playing at Charley's would bring the old magic back but it wasn't happening. The folks out there seemed to have enjoyed it but a music exec would have noticed those screw-ups – and written her off after the first song.

After splashing her face and running her damp hands over her hair in a largely futile attempt to tame the halo of frizz that had sprouted there, she stepped back into the hall. She should return to the main room to greet her "fans" – the locals who had come to gawk – but she needed another minute alone. She followed the red glow of the exit sign, and slipped out the back. The door didn't close all the way, and laughter and the hum of conversation followed her out to the moonlit parking lot. After the closeness of the bar, the mountain breeze felt cool against her skin. She removed her vest, then leaned forward, and lifted her hair to let the air caress her nape.

She was straightening up when she saw it. Moonlight glinted off gray metal. A bug-eye headlight stared straight ahead. Handlebars curved back over the silvery tank, pointing in invitation to the leather seat. A classic Harley Fat Boy. Sexy, powerful. Familiar. It was the same kind of motorcycle as the one she'd seen in Nashville.

She glanced around, then stepped towards it, reaching out to touch the cool chrome. She trailed her hand along the leather seat, and closed her eyes. A shudder rippled through her that had little to do with the coolness of the air, and her heartbeat picked up a notch. Whether from the memories stirred by the bike, knowing he was near or both, she couldn't tell. Because there was no question of whom this bike belonged to.

Ty Monroe was around here somewhere. Contrary to what she'd told Rob, deep down she'd known there was a possibility that he would still be in town. Why else would she have stayed away for so long?

Memories invaded her mind, flowing from the touch of her hand on the leather. Riding this bike had been like sex itself: her breasts pressed against his back, her thighs gripping his, the powerful vibrations of the engine between her legs. Moist heat pooled in her panties, and she took a deep breath.

"Welcome home."

The voice had played so many times inside her head that it took a moment for her to realize that it was coming from behind her. She jerked her hand back, and whirled around.

A tall figure stood between her and the door. A light-colored button-down stretched over a muscled torso, tucked loosely into dark blue jeans. A few dark curls peeked out the top where the button was undone. Creases bracketed his mouth, reminders of what his full lips could do. When her gaze reached his eyes, they were in shadow but she knew they were a pale, wintry blue.

Just like that the time and distance fell away, leaving her as vulnerable as the naive young woman who'd bolted three years ago. She hoped it was dark enough to hide the heat that rose in her cheeks. A familiar panic fluttered in her chest, accompanied by an ache in her womb, and she looked away, reminding herself to breathe.

Seconds ticked by. With a deep exhale she regained some measure of composure, and turned back. Ty opened his mouth but she spoke first, gesturing behind her. "Nice bike." Inside, she cringed. She'd pictured this scene a hundred times, and the best she could come up with was "nice bike"? It was the same damned bike he'd always had.

Lame, Ashley. Really lame.

He stepped closer, and she looked up, finally meeting that steady gaze. He'd always been tall but seemed to take up even more space than she remembered. She was glad the bike prevented her from stepping back, and revealing how off-balance she felt.

One corner of his mouth tilted up. "Wanna go for a ride?"

The question was both invitation and challenge. That she knew better than to rise to the bait this time didn't stop the reaction that his words evoked. Her inner muscles clenched, and her nipples tightened. A downward flicker of his eyes belied her hope that he hadn't noticed her body's response – she could only pray that he attributed it to the cool evening air.

Blue flames flared in his eyes, and a muscle ticked in his jaw. Perhaps she wasn't the only one affected by this exchange.

"I have to go back in." She nodded at the door. "For another song."

She hadn't planned to sing any more but Ty's proximity was making her brain go fuzzy, which meant it was time to put this little reunion to an end before she did something stupid. She glanced at the exit. Before he could react, she slipped around him and through the door, tossing a whispered "bye" over her shoulder.

She paused in the corridor, and leaned against the wall. Her breath came in soft pants, like she'd run a race. After a moment of silence she heard a sharp curse and the rev of an engine, followed by the sound of a motorcycle disappearing into the night.

♫

Rob took a sip of his beer and surveyed the crowd. The Heartbreak Hillbillies' release party was in full swing. People milled about with drinks in their hands, and the band's latest album played over the sound system, competing with the laughter and conversation that swirled around the room. Musicians rubbed elbows with agents who could advance their careers. Recording label execs looked for the next big thing to fill their coffers. Everywhere he looked beautiful people preened and planned, plotting their rise to international stardom.

Rob was exhausted just watching it.

Across the room he spotted a brunette in a miniskirt who looked vaguely familiar. Was she one of the girls in Grant's latest video? No, it was Jackson's, for that sexy song about "slipping between the sheets." At that thought another face popped into his mind, one with sleepy green eyes and tousled red hair above a sheet pulled up to the chin. Ashley. He smiled to himself.

The brunette must have taken his smile as encouragement – she peeked at him from under the curtain of her hair, and pulled her shoulders back, accentuating unnaturally round breasts that threatened to bust out of her low-cut top.

Nice, if you were into that sort of thing. He wasn't. He took a quick sip of his drink and looked away. His gaze landing on the back of a tall, muscular man in a Stetson and faded jeans. Now, that was more to his taste. Rob looked him over, and the other man turned, tilting his hat in Rob's direction. Recognition dawned. Kyle. Did lighting or some other backstage thing. They'd hooked up a number of times last year but Rob had pulled back when it became apparent that the other man was interested in more than sex. Rob only did casual.

Kyle's brows went up in obvious question, but Rob shook his head. The other man gave him a "can't-fault-me-for-trying" shrug, and turned to thread his way into the crowd.

Rob let out an exasperated breath. A room full of beautiful people and booze, and he was nursing a beer in the shadows. Alone. He liked the folks in the Hillbillies – he should be enjoying their party. Or at least taking advantage of the crowd. With Ashley out of commission, it was even more important for him to be out there. Mingling. Getting his name and face in front of Nashville bigwigs could mean the difference between getting a second album for Sweet Talk or heading back to Texas to work the oil rigs like his brother. Instead, he was hanging out alone in a corner.

He downed the rest of his drink, and set the bottle on the shelf behind him. He wasn't going to impress anyone with the mood he was in, so he might as well head home. He was reaching into his wallet to grab a few bills for the waitress when a firm hand landed on his shoulder.

"Rob! Good to see you here, man." Brad stood before him, a glass of amber liquid in his hand. "Let me get you a drink."

Before Rob could protest that he was on his way out, Brad had caught the bartender's eye, and raised his glass. Rob hesitated for a moment, then leaned back against the wall with a shrug. Why not? All he had to go home to was an empty apartment.

A waitress arrived with a tray. She handed him a glass, and he smiled his thanks. He took an experimental sip. Bourbon. Top shelf. Brad had expensive taste. The waitress reached around Rob to retrieve his empty beer bottle from the shelf. He kept his eyes on his glass, pretending not to notice when her breast rubbed against his arm.

"Anything else I can get for you boys?"

Rob shook his head. She paused for a moment, then turned

with a pout and stalked away. When he was sure she that was gone, Rob looked up. Brad was following the progress of her tiny shorts with interest.

Brad turned back to Rob with a smile, and pointed towards the entrance. "The stacked chick by the door was checking you out too."

Rob shrugged. Over the other man's shoulder, he could see the brunette from the video now displaying her impressive wares to one of the male members of the band.

"The guy behind her, too." There was less admiration in Brad's voice this time.

Rob raised a brow, and stared at Brad until the other man turned away. Shortly after they'd signed with Brad, Rob had discovered that their manager wasn't comfortable with Rob's interest in men. Brad feared that the conservative country music crowd – specifically, the record executives – would never accept an openly gay or bi male singer. To Rob, Brad's mercenary attitude was somehow worse than simple homophobia. The fact that he was probably right only pissed Rob off more.

Brad looked around. "So where's Ashley?"

"Went home for a couple of days to visit her grandma."

Brad nodded. "Good for her. It'll do her some good to have downtime before the next show."

Ashley had said almost the same thing, but Rob felt his hackles rise anyway. "Ashley hasn't been home to visit her grandma in a while. The woman is getting on in years."

Brad nodded. When no more was said about Ashley's absence, Rob relaxed muscles he hadn't been aware of tensing, and took another sip of his drink. From over the rim of his glass, he watched his manager. Brad had ditched his usual jacket and tie for a plaid button-down with pearl buttons and jeans, and leaned casually against the wall, but Rob could see his dark eyes scanning the room. Looking for the "right" person to schmooze with, no doubt. Brad had a great reputation for helping bands get noticed, but something about the man rubbed Rob the wrong way.

He gave himself a mental shake. Brad was talented and hungry, and worked hard. He'd promised some big "opportunities" for Sweet Talk during his one-year trial contract, which would end in a few weeks. If his approach seemed more aggressive lately, that was a good thing, right?

Brad turned back his way, but before he could point out someone for Rob to suck up – talk to, Rob spoke. "So, how's the recording deal coming along?"

"It's pretty good." Brad tipped his head towards the suits by the stage. "I've got leads on some small labels like this one. I'll feel them out over the next few weeks, and send them your stuff." Brad looked down at his glass as he swirled the amber liquid. "That's one way to go of course, but those guys are always a risk. Could go belly-up like your last label."

Rob nodded. Their first album had done pretty well but it hadn't been enough to keep the small struggling house from going under, leaving Sweet Talk to find another deal.

Brad looked up. The calculation in his eye had ratcheted up a dozen notches. "There's another possibility I want to discuss with you."

Something in his tone made Rob tense up again. "You mentioned that you wanted to talk the other day. Unless it's something that has to be decided now, the three of us can chat on Monday, when Ashley is back in town."

While it wasn't unusual for him or Ashley to speak for Sweet Talk without the other being around, Rob's gut was telling him that this wasn't a conversation he wanted to have right now. Maybe it was the weird mood he was in tonight. If so, it was past time to blow this joint. He raised his glass to his lips, ignoring Brad's wince as he tossed back the rest of the expensive liquor in one gulp.

Brad spoke. "Actually, I was hoping to talk to you alone."

"About what?" Rob didn't bother to keep the suspicion from his voice.

If Brad heard his tone, he ignored it. "Seems like Ashley's been having a rough time. I mean, between you and me, she hasn't been playing very well lately."

Brad's expression was sympathetic, but Rob was wary. "Everyone has a bad day from time to time."

Brad raised a brow. "But it's been more than a day hasn't it? She hasn't had a good performance for months now, and the reviewers are taking notice. What did the Music City Paper say?"

Rob held up a hand before Brad could repeat the damning words. "Critics look for any reason to tear musicians down, and that bitch is the worst."

"But she wasn't the only one, and the labels are starting to notice. I was hoping to get you guys onstage for the opening of that new club, but the booking agent balked after she read those reviews."

"Then we don't need them. There will be other shows."

"Rob," Brad said shaking his head. "Your loyalty is commendable but—"

Rob clenched his fists to keep himself from wiping the patronizing smile off Brad's face. "My loyalty is to my partner and the other half of the act that you represent – at least for the next couple of weeks."

Brad raised his hands in a conciliatory gesture but his eyes had gone hard. "Hey, no need for that. It's my job to look out for you two – together and as individuals – and I'd be failing if I didn't admit that I was concerned. Your support of Ashley is admirable, but it won't get either of you a contract."

Rob gritted his teeth. What could he say? Brad was only spelling out what Ashley had been saying for weeks. So why did it feel disloyal to even listen to the other man's words?

Brad continued. "It sounds like you guys had a good session yesterday, and that's a start. I'll keep doing what I can to get you guys gigs and a recording deal, okay?" He held out a hand.

Rob hesitated for a moment. Brad was doing what he had to do. What they'd hired him to do. Pushing aside his distaste, Rob shook the other's man's hand.

Brad finished his drink with more appreciation than Rob had shown for the bourbon, and set his glass on the table. He tilted his head, as if gauging Rob's mood. "There's something else I want to talk to you about..." Rob's eyes narrowed, "but it can wait."

Rob nodded. It was long past time for him to get out of there. He tossed a few bills on the table and headed for the door.

Chapter Five

Sunshine poured through the lace curtains, and the sound of a broom swept in from the porch below, but it was the tantalizing promise of coffee that convinced Ashley to open her eyes and face the bittersweet reality of being back home.

For the first time in years, those icy blue eyes hadn't been a dream. She'd seen Ty Monroe in the flesh last night, and the imprint of those few minutes had made it impossible to sleep. For hours she'd tossed and turned, her mind blending memory with a generous sprinkling of fantasy until she couldn't close her eyes without seeing his face. Hearing his voice. Feeling his body against hers.

Her first love. Her first heartbreak. Of course she'd run into him on her first night back.

She sighed. Other than that, the night had been pretty good. She hadn't needed the repeated cries of *encore* or the compliments of the locals to tell her that her second set – the one she hadn't planned to play – had been good. Not as good as she'd been before her slump, but better than she'd been lately. And a hell of a lot better than she'd been when she'd left town three years ago.

It figured that Ty had missed that set. What would he have thought if he'd heard her? Would he have realized that he'd been wrong?

Ty had been her rock from the moment she met him. Smart. Serious. And so damned sexy. He never laughed at her dream of becoming a country star, only encouraged her to be her best. So naturally, he was the first person she went to with her big news the night of the county fair. Rob Porter had heard her sing, and invited her to replace his back-up singer for the last leg of their tour. It was the chance she'd been praying for – an opportunity to learn the ropes from a real country band. But instead of being happy for her, Ty had launched into a litany of reasons why she shouldn't go. How she wasn't ready. Unspoken in his arguments was an ultimatum: him or Rob. Love or the chance to make her Nashville dream come true.

A man who truly loved her would never have forced her to make that choice. Three years had passed but the realization still stung.

She shook her head to clear it. Ty Monroe had already taken up far too much of her time and energy. Until she could put some real distance between them again, it was best to put him out of her mind.

She sat up in bed, and slipped her feet to the floor. Footsteps approached the bottom of the steps. "Ashley honey, are you up?"

"Yes, Granny! Be down in a minute." After pulling on a tee and a pair of shorts Ashley stumbled down the stairs, and followed the welcoming sounds and smells of frying bacon to the kitchen. Granny stood by the counter pouring milk into a large purple mug until the brew was the perfect shade of caramel that Ashley loved. She handed the mug to Ashley, and turned back to tend the frying pan on the stove.

Ashley took a generous sip, then put the mug down. She came up behind the older woman, gently slipping her arms around her waist. Granny's bony shoulder was sharp beneath her cheek and as comforting as a favorite pair of slippers. "Mornin', Granny."

"Ashley, dear." The words resonated under Ashley's ear. She kissed the flower-print-covered shoulder, and stepped out of the way to allow Granny to maneuver two fried eggs onto a plate.

Ashley turned towards the table. It was covered with the usual flowered cloth and crowded with dishes. Eggs, biscuits, gravy and, of course, coffee. Since Granny was an early riser and would have already eaten, the spread was meant for Ashley. She shook her head with a smile. Rob would be pleased to see her eating so well. He was always after her to eat, saying she could use a little more meat on her bones whenever she protested.

Her face flushed. She'd never thought that Rob noticed what she looked like, but after his offer the other night... She gulped a mouthful of coffee, and moved towards the counter, hoping that Granny wouldn't notice her suddenly red cheeks.

A postcard was stuck on the fridge. It must have come this morning because it hadn't been there when Ashley arrived yesterday. The front showed three men in cowboy hats and chaps pointing guitars at the camera like they were shotguns under the name *The Sidekicks*. Words across the bottom announced that they were playing the Starstruck Lounge in Oklahoma in two weeks time.

She flipped the card over. *Dear Momma – Carlton's band is doing great! He's got another gig after this one, and we're hopeful that it'll lead to something big. Keep your fingers crossed! How are you? I hope all is well. Give my love to Ashley. XOXO – Darlene.*

Ashley turned towards Granny, and held up the card. "So Carlton's going places. Again." She shook her head. "She's ten times more talented than he is. I don't get how she can be content to live in his shadow."

Granny shrugged. "Your mama's different, child. She never had your desire to succeed. Your passion."

Ashley snorted. "She has passion, alright. She just throws it away on men instead of focusing it on her music."

Granny's eyes narrowed, and her hands went to her hips. "That's no way to speak about your mama, Ashley Ford, and you know it."

Ashley hung her head. "Sorry, Granny." Regardless of what Mama had done, it hurt Granny's feelings when Ashley talked like that, and Mama had hurt Granny too much already.

Granny shook her head, and smiled. "Your mama's not like you, Ashley dear. It's enough for her to be around music without making it herself. Besides, she's happy with Carlton."

Ashley couldn't imagine being satisfied with that but, since it wasn't fair to put Granny in the middle, she let it drop. Mama had ceased to be a major force in Ashley's life when she'd deposited her only daughter on Granny's doorstep ten years ago. Ashley wasn't going to waste time arguing about the woman now.

Still, the postcard had been a good reminder. After seeing her mama's musical ambitions take a back seat to a succession of boyfriends, Ashley had vowed not to let romance interfere with her own goals. Rob would never be able to understand her "celibacy" – he needed sex like other people needed food – but Ashley had seen how relationships could suck the creative energy out of a woman. She would not let the same thing happen to her, although she'd once come close with Ty Monroe.

Ashley returned to the table with her coffee. Granny patted her hand. "Speaking of musical passion, I heard wonderful things about your performance last night, dear. The whole town is buzzing."

Ashley looked at the clock that hung on the far wall. Not even ten o'clock, and Granny had already heard the gossip. That was small town life. "I hadn't planned to do it, but I'm glad I did. It was fun." She snorted. "It was Val's idea, of course."

"I should have known," Granny said, but her eyes were smiling. Even though Val had had a bit of a wild reputation, Granny had always encouraged Ashley's friendship with the other girl. Said Val was *good balance* for Ashley, whatever that meant.

"Did you see a lot of old friends?"

She wouldn't call them friends, per se. She shrugged. "There were some familiar faces. Luke, Sally Anne, Carlton." She looked into her cup, and swallowed, fighting her curiosity about a certain someone. She lost. "Oh, and Ty was there."

"Was he?"

She glanced up at Granny's tone but her face held only an expression of mild interest. Ashley fought to keep her tone equally mild. "I thought Ty left town when his folks retired. I heard he sold the construction business."

"And bought Charley's with his part of the sale."

"What?" Ty owned Charley's. Funny that Val had neglected to mention that small fact.

"He's been running Charley's since you left, although from what I hear he's hardly ever there. Don't know what the boy has been up to but he seems to spend a lot of time out of town these days."

Out of town? Could that have been Ty's Harley she'd seen the other day? She dismissed the thought as soon as it arose. While Ty's bike was unique in Oak Valley, it couldn't be the only one like that in all of Nashville. In fact, it was the kind of classic American motorcycle you'd expect a Nashville good 'ole boy to covet.

Besides, what would Ty have been doing on Music Row?

Rob prowled from room to room. *Where was his damned phone?* He remembered taking it out when he got in last night, and usually put it on his dresser, but it wasn't there. What had he done with it? He checked the bathroom counter and the kitchen, the mantle and coffee table. The dining room table. Everywhere he could have put it...

He spun on his heel, and headed back down the hall, turning into Ashley's room. There it was, sitting on her bedside table.

He'd stopped in her room last night when he'd gotten in. The sight of her neatly made bed had made him feel – what exactly? He shook his head, and looked down at his phone, flicking through his call history. *Damn.* He'd called her when he'd gotten in at one a.m. He'd been pissed off after his conversation with Brad, and missing her, and... He shook his head. He hadn't been thinking clearly. Seemed like that happened a lot where Ashley was concerned. Good thing her phone had been off.

And good thing she'd taken some time for herself. Maybe this slump she was going through was hitting her harder than he realized. All artists went through bad periods. He should know – he'd been deep in one himself when he met Ashley.

He smiled. The moment he'd seen her at that county fair, singing her heart out on a rickety wooden stage, he'd known she was something special. Her voice, her passion. There was no doubt in his mind they were meant to sing together. Sure enough, as soon as she'd joined him, his career had started looking up. They'd formed Sweet Talk, and recorded their first album six months later. She was good for him. No, she was the best-damned thing that had ever happened to him.

Rob leaned against the wall, and stared up at the ceiling fan. *Ashley*. Over the past three years they'd become more than friends. They worked together. They lived together. Hell, they were practically married except for the physical part, and like an idiot he'd offered to change that the other night. Not that he'd meant it.

Who was he kidding? Of course he'd meant it, and would have been fucking ecstatic if she'd said yes, but he still couldn't believe he'd let his guard down enough to actually say it. Good thing she'd assumed it was a joke.

Yeah, good thing.

Still, three years was a long time to go without having sex. He knew that her ex had broken her heart, but shouldn't she be over that by now? And didn't she miss sex?

Maybe that was the real reason he didn't go for women – they didn't make any sense.

But damn, would it be good between us. He licked his lips. She was everything a man could want – a lush ripe body wrapped in a hot little package. And that red hair – from catching her in the shower Rob knew she had red hair down there too. He reached down to adjust his cock, which had swelled in his jeans. To be honest, *that's* what he'd been thinking about when he called her last night, and he hadn't even been drunk. Thank God, she hadn't answered – he would have made a fool of himself. Again.

Hey, Ashley, I was calling to offer myself for some sexual healing. I know you're frustrated, and I've wanted you for years, so why not screw? Yeah, that would have gone over real well – and totally fucked up the best relationship he'd ever had.

He hit his head with the heel of his hand. Sometimes he could be so fucking stupid.

He left Ashley's room, thumbing through his messages. Ashley had left him a voicemail earlier this morning. "Hi Rob! I see you called me at one a.m. Back from the Hillbillies' party, right? I hope you had a good time."

Rob thought about his conversation with Brad and snarled. The party would have been much better with Ashley there.

The message continued. "Anyway, you won't believe it – I played at the local bar last night. It was Val's idea. And you know what? I wasn't too bad. My second set was actually pretty good."

There was a pause. "Um, guess who I ran into." Rob heard her take a deep breath, and held his own, fearing what she would say next. "My ex." She sighed. "After all this time..." Her voice trailed off.

Damn it, he knew something like this was going to happen. Ty Monroe was the last person Ashley needed to deal with right now. She was going through a rough patch, doubting her talent and future. She didn't need anyone reinforcing those doubts.

When Rob invited Ashley to join his act, her then-boyfriend Ty had argued against it. Claimed that she couldn't make it. Wasn't ready. She'd cried for months afterward. Given that she'd hardly dated in the three years since then, Rob suspected that she'd never gotten over the guy. Just pushed the hurt down deep enough that she could ignore it.

He replayed her message. She started out okay, happy even, and then... she sounded lost. Defeated. As if just seeing Ty made her feel that way. Rob shook his head. They couldn't afford another setback. Too much was riding on Ashley getting her groove back. On Rob getting Ashley back – as a singing partner, if nothing else. With a curse, he stuffed his phone in his pocket, and stormed out of the room.

There was no way he was going to let that bastard hurt her again.

Chapter Six

Ashley wrestled with the box of food on the passenger seat of her car. Granny hadn't been able to resist sending her to the barbecue with a "little something," which translated into three-dozen homemade hamburger buns and enough peach cobbler to feed a small village. Ashley shifted the box, and grabbed a bag from the floor of her car. Val had texted her with a request to get more ice, so she was carrying that too.

With the box held against her middle, she followed the noise coming from behind the house, trying not to whack herself with the bag of ice. She reached the high wooden gate that led to the back deck, and turned, trying to bump it open with her butt. It didn't budge.

"Can someone get the gate? My hands are full."

No answer. She raised her voice to be heard over the music. "Can I get a hand here?" The box was digging into her belly. She shifted her hands to get a better grip, and the bag of ice slid to the ground.

After a moment, the gate creaked open behind her. Ashley reached down to snag the handle of the plastic bag. With everything balanced she straightened, and turned – right into the most beautiful male body she'd ever laid eyes on.

Broad shoulders filled her view. Smooth, hard muscles flowed down to a solid chest. Dark hair surrounded two flat bronze nipples that made her teeth itch with the urge to bite. She licked her lips. Some part of her brain registered that this pectoral specimen looked familiar, but she pushed the warning away. Her gaze moved south along a narrow trail of hair to a taut six-pack. Her core muscles tightened in appreciation. The sight of a pale scar on the right side of that flat stomach raised another red flag, but the hint went unheeded in favor of continuing along that path of sin to the bulge that hung below the waistband of a pair of dark blue jeans. Her eyes widened as she watched it swell.

"See anything you like?"

Mental alarm bells finally pierced her consciousness, and she stumbled back. Her gaze flew up to meet a familiar ice blue stare and a mocking smile that did nothing to diminish the kissability of those lips. Heat flamed into her cheeks. With no thought except escape, she dropped the ice, and shoved the box into his midsection. He grabbed it with sharp exhale. She scrambled back to the car, gravel skittering beneath her feet. She yanked the handle open, dove in, and pulled the door shut behind her.

Damn. Her heart raced. She took a few deep breaths, but her fingers still trembled, and her core muscles twitched. All because of a three-second scan of Ty's bare chest. *Damn, damn, damn.* He'd always provoked out-of-control feelings in her, and she hated that. She'd never admitted it, but it was one of the main reasons she'd avoided coming home for so long.

Her hands were still cold from handling the ice, and she held them up to her burning cheeks. Ty was Val's brother's friend

– how could Ashley have not realized that he would be here? More importantly, why was Ashley still so susceptible to him? Nashville was full of men more beautiful than he, international superstars worshipped by millions. None had ever made her act as stupid as she did around Ty Monroe.

She slumped against the seat – she so didn't need this right now. She'd come home to escape from one insane attraction, and here she was running from another. What was wrong with her?

Maybe she should head back to Granny's – tell Val that she was feeling stressed, and needed to rest before the show. She grimaced. Like that would convince her friend. Val would probably head over to Granny's right in the middle of the party to haul her ass back. For her own good, of course. Better to head back to Nashville today, and call Val from the road. No, that wouldn't work – Granny was expecting her to stick around until tomorrow.

Okay, so all she had to do was avoid Ty until she could slip away tomorrow morning.

She sat up. What was she thinking? The "great love" she'd imagined with Ty was over, good riddance, never coming back. Yes, she was still attracted to him – *strongly* attracted – but surely she could manage to act like a normal human being around him for a little while. After all, she was attracted to Rob and managed to keep that under control. More or less.

Maybe that wasn't the best argument for this little pep talk.

She sat up. She was twenty-two years old, not some kid with a crush. She could handle this. She just had to stop staring at Ty like a dog in heat. And regardless of how stupid she felt, she couldn't hide in the driveway any longer. She'd be hard-pressed to explain why she was sitting in her car, and with the windows rolled up and the A/C off, it was getting hot in here.

She took a deep breath, straightened her shoulders and reached for the door handle. This was her hometown too – she would not let Ty chase her away again.

Ty sat on the edge of a lounge chair, gripping a beer in his hand, and trying to relax. But his gaze was fixed on the path from the gate. He knew he should accept the inevitable – that she'd fled from him *again* – but he stared at the side of the house as if he could will her to come around the corner. At least he hadn't heard a car start so she was still out there.

A sharp ping and a curse drew his attention to the massive gas grill that squatted on the deck. Luke, Val's older brother, had brought it over from their parents' house only to discover that it was broken. He'd been trying to fix the thing for a half hour. From the sounds coming from beneath it, it was hard to tell if he was making progress.

Ty turned back to the gate in time to see Ashley slip into the yard, her feet barely making a sound on the flagstones. She scanned the group, her gaze skimming over him before alighting on the group clustered at the far end of the deck. His teeth clenched. *She'd been looking plenty a few minutes ago.*

Ty wasn't the only one who noticed her entrance. With a quick glance at him, Val leapt from her chair. "Ashley. I was wondering if you were going to come on back, or just drop off the ice and leave."

Every head turned in response to Val's words. Ashley blushed, and shrugged the tote bag slung over one shoulder. "I, um, forgot my bag in the car."

Val grabbed Ashley by the wrist, as if she didn't trust her friend to stay, and pulled her over to the cluster. Val waved at the people on the deck chairs, who were now sitting up a bit straighter. "I think you know most of the people here, but there are a few new faces, too."

The people Val pointed to were locals, folks who had known Ashley for years. Still, they wore slightly star-struck expressions on their faces, and brightened when she smiled back. Ashley gave them all a little wave. "Hi y'all."

Two men at the edge of the group had risen from their chairs when Ashley came over, and now moved closer to Val, clearly looking for introductions. One of them, Tom Bennett, was a former classmate of Ty's who'd returned from the Army to run his parents' hardware store. The other guy was unfamiliar but his blond hair and pretty boy looks reminded Ty of the singer Ashley had run off with. He resisted an urge to growl.

Val gestured to them. "Ashley, I don't know if you know Tom. He was a few years ahead of us, so he might have joined the Army before you came to town. Maybe you met over the summer?"

Tom held out a hand, which Ashley shook with a smile. "No, I've never had the pleasure of meeting Oak Valley's famous singing sensation. Really bad timing on my part."

Ty had never had anything against Tom, but the subtle head-to-toe Tom gave Ashley made him want to shove the guy into the deep end of the pool.

Val gestured to the other man. "This is Tom's cousin, Roy. He's visiting from Atlanta. Just finished law school, and is spending the summer with Tom's family while he studies for the bar."

Ashley turned to Roy. "Pleased to meet you. I'm Ashley

Ford."

She held out her hand. Roy took it but instead of shaking it he leaned over, and placed a kiss on the back. Ashley's eyes widened. "The pleasure is mine, Miss Ford," he said as he straightened. Ty found himself rising from his seat, only settling down when Ashley pulled her hand back.

A satisfied grunt sounded from the other end of the deck. Luke rose up from behind the grill, brushing his hands on his shorts. "There, the fuel line is fixed, and the tray is clean – ready for another summer's worth of good eating." He rubbed his hands together. "Now, we can fire up this baby, and I'll make some of my famous Coleman burgers."

Val turned to him, and laughed. "*Infamous* Coleman burgers. Or maybe you meant c-o-a-l? Last time they were so black and hard, we could have used them to heat the grill."

"It wasn't my fault the grill caught on fire – the hose was defective." He wagged a finger at his sister. "The gas line is now clear, and working just fine, so be nice to the chef or you'll be eating take-out. But first I'm going for a swim." He wiped his brow, streaking it with dirt. "It's damned hot out here!"

Val's eyes widened. "You best get that black stuff off you before you even think about getting in my pool, Luke Coleman!" She had a point – Luke's arms were black to the elbows, and streaks of soot decorated his legs.

Luke laughed. With a "yes, ma'am" and a mocking bow towards his sister, he headed towards the house. Ashley's gaze followed him to the back doors, and Ty felt an uncharacteristic stab of jealousy towards his friend. A moment later she turned to Val, and pointed a thumb towards the house. "The pool sounds like a good idea. I'll go change into my suit."

Val nodded. "There's sunscreen in the hall bathroom."

Ashley spun around, heading for the sliding glass doors. She scrambled across the deck, and Ty's gaze was drawn to her tiny cutoff shorts, which hugged her ass like a second skin. He let out a slow breath. If she came out in a bikini, he wasn't sure he could be held responsible for his actions. He looked over to where the others were sitting. Every male gaze was locked on the same view. Roy elbowed Tom in the ribs, nodding towards where Ashley had disappeared.

A muscle ticked in Ty's jaw, and he rose from his chair. Maybe he should change into his suit, too – it was hot and a swim would be the thing to cool him down. That's what he told himself as he picked his bag up, and followed Luke and Ashley's path into the house.

He stepped through the glass sliding door, and squinted into the dim interior. He walked through the kitchen and into the hall, pausing outside the closed bathroom door. He heard the sound of movement, and water.

Was Ashley on the other side of the door, slipping out of those tiny shorts? Ty's mouth went dry. A vision of Ashley performing a slow strip tease popped into his mind, and his balls drew up tight. What would she do if he opened the door? Slap him across the face – or pull him into an empty bedroom? She'd always been wild in bed, tearing at his clothes, and making little impatient sounds when he kissed her. Touched her. *Licked* her. His cock hardened.

Laughter from outside interrupted his fantasy. *What the hell am I thinking?* This was the woman who'd left without even a good-bye, and had refused his calls for weeks. His texts had gone unanswered. Her return changed nothing. He turned away from the door in disgust.

Ty located an empty guest bedroom, and closed the door

behind him, turning the lock with a click. If only he could lock her out of his thoughts as easily. He caught a glimpse of his frustrated expression in the mirror above the low dresser. Those cutoffs had exposed an indecent amount of leg, gripping her ass as tightly as he'd wanted to when she bent over in front of him at the gate. But it was the way she'd looked at every other male there, while avoiding his eyes that made what little blood that had not hightailed it to his groin pound between his ears.

Of course, she was all smiles for Tom and that smarmy lawyer Roy. Even Luke warranted a second look. But Ty? Aside from their encounter at the gate, she'd done a pretty good job of pretending he didn't exist. He couldn't say the same – his cock had responded to her presence like a lodestone to the North Pole. He was so hard, it hurt.

He reached down to adjust himself, trying to ease the pressure of his jeans on his dick. Maybe he should take a cold shower. Not that the earlier one had helped.

Well, damn. He couldn't go out there like this, and no man had the power to will an erection like this down in less than an hour. He had to take care of this himself or knock on the bathroom door – and that wasn't happening.

Maybe getting off, even by his own hand, would calm his blood enough to allow him to get through this party. To survive seeing Ashley in nothing more than a skimpy bathing suit... Another pulse of blood rushed south. His thoughts were not helping matters. He exhaled in a rush. Is this is what he'd been reduced to – hiding in a bedroom jerking himself off because of Ashley Ford? He shook his head. He never should have come to Val's. Never should have tempted fate.

Too late now.

Chapter Seven

Ashley pulled the metallic blue tankini top over her breasts, and tugged it down until only a sliver of her midriff was exposed. She stepped into the bottoms, smoothed down her hair, and slipped into her flip-flops. She still needed to put on sunscreen – she couldn't afford to get sunburned the day before a show. Luke had been showering in the hall bathroom when she'd come in, so she'd had to use the one attached to the guest rooms instead. He was probably done by now, so she could grab the sunscreen on the way out.

She checked her hair. Fiddled with the tankini straps. Checked her back view in the mirror. When she turned on the faucet to wash her hands for the second time, she had to admit that she was stalling. Putting off the moment that she'd have to face Ty.

All the work she'd put into forgetting him? All the defenses she'd erected during those first lonely months in Nashville? Gone. Lost in a heartbeat at the gate. No, they'd had crumbled the moment she'd spotted his bike outside of Charley's last night. Then she'd caught sight of those blue eyes, and she'd been right back where they'd left off – as if minutes had passed since their last touch, not years.

She braced her hands on the sink and looked at herself in the mirror. Her face was flushed, eyes bright with arousal. Her skin tingled, and her belly clenched.

She exhaled, and shook her head. She didn't need this on top of everything else she was dealing with – didn't need the doubts he reinforced, didn't need the crazy feelings he provoked. She'd left all that behind, and for good reason, so there was no reason need to put up with it now. She'd grab a burger, chat for a few minutes with Val, and put Ty behind her once more. For good.

With that resolution in mind, she opened the bathroom door, looking down to check her new tankini top once more. Maybe she should put the shorts back on. An anguished groan sounded right in front of her. She looked up, and her mouth dropped open.

Ty stood in the middle of the room, turned slightly away from her, feet planted wide apart. His head was thrown back, his eyes were closed, and his breath hissed out from between clenched teeth. His erect cock jutted out of his open shorts, and his fist wrapped around its base. As she watched, he slowly stroked the length of his erection. Up and down. Up and down. Her breath caught in her throat. Heat flared between her thighs, and muscles clenched deep in her core. It was the most erotic thing she had ever seen.

A guttural sound issued from Ty's throat, and memories flooded her mind like an X-rated multi-media show. Ty's face above her as he thrust hard and fast. The rough hair of his legs between her thighs as she straddled him. His breath on her ear as he entered her from behind.

He stroked himself again, and her hand clenched involuntarily, remembering the feel of that velvet-covered steel in her fist. A wave of pure lust shot through her, forcing the breath from her lungs with a gasp. Her tote bag dropped to the floor.

Ty's head whipped around. His face was flushed, and his nostrils flared like a beast scenting prey. Arousal and fear swept through her, but she couldn't look away. In two steps, he was before of her. Another two and he had crowded her against the wall. Her knees buckled, and he caught her, his hands grabbing her ass.

Her breasts pressed against his chest as he pulled her closer. The tip of his cock grazed the bare skin above her waistband, and she shivered with pleasure. Some part of her knew this was crazy but she couldn't stop. Years of deprivation overwhelmed her, and rational thought fled. After missing him for so long, she could no sooner pull away than refuse to take her next breath.

His mouth came down on hers, hot and demanding. His tongue swept between her lips, sweeping her inhibitions away. She arched against him. She needed this. She needed more. She needed Ty. Here. *Now.*

Her hands traveled up his body, and fisted in his hair. With a feral growl, one hand left her ass, and moved around to her ribs, slipping down to the edge of the tankini top. He grabbed the hem, and pulled it up until her breasts sprang free. He cupped the underside of one mound, stroking the tender skin of her areola with his thumb.

There was no thought, only sensation. Ty's hand on her breast, the other on her ass. His cock against her middle. An emptiness deep in her womb, aching to be filled. She whimpered, mad with need, and Ty's hand closed, pinching her nipple between his thumb and forefinger. She moaned again. She couldn't see the triumph in his gaze, but she could feel it in his smile when his lips curved against hers. She didn't care – she was *beyond* caring –

her whole being reduced to the desire that drove her.

She writhed in his arms, urging him on with her body. He seemed to get the hint. While his lips continued their assault on hers, the hand that had gripped her breast journeyed down to her waist, grazing the skin inside the elastic of her swimsuit bottoms. A spike of pleasure lanced through her to her clit, and her inner muscles pulsed in erotic Morse code. *Yes. More. Now.* She bucked against him, and he answered by grinding his hips into hers. The base of his cock pushed her sensitive clit, and she cried out. *More. Yes. Please.*

Ty caught the elastic waistband with his thumb, and pulled it down her thighs with a jerk. The scent of her arousal rose between them. He groaned, and cupped her mound, slipping one finger between her swollen lips. His finger grazed her nub. Pleasure spiked through her, and her whole body trembled.

"*Ashley.*"

Her name was a plea on his lips, and she nodded her assent. Whatever it was that he wanted, she would give it to him without reservation because she wanted it too. He stepped sideways, taking them both to the low dresser. When his hand left her pussy, she moaned at the loss. With a chuckle, he reached into his back pocket, pulled out his wallet, and tossed it onto the wooden surface beside them. Still gripping her ass, he fumbled with it one-handed until he found a shiny square packet. Prize in hand, he swept his arm across the top of the dresser, flinging the wallet and everything else to the floor.

He grabbed her hips, and lifted her onto the smooth, cool surface. Faced with his strong hard chest, she gave into her earlier impulse and took that flat nipple into her mouth. She nipped it, and felt a shudder rock his body.

He yanked her swimsuit bottoms down her legs, tossing

them aside while her hands swept down his back. She pushed his jeans and boxers down to pool at his feet. She caressed his now-bare ass and the muscles along his sides. *Long and strong.* That's how she'd always though of Ty. Tall, lean body. Strong, elegant hands. Long, hard cock.

His mouth dropped to her throat. She tipped her head back to allow him greater access, and he nipped at the sensitive tendons that stood out where her shoulder joined her neck. Tremors raced through her, resonating in her core like a clanging of a gong. She wrapped her legs tightly around his waist, pulling him to her, forcing his hardness against her soft, wet pussy.

Ty's lips left her throat. He looked down at her, his eyes questioning but narrowed, as if daring her to deny her their obvious passion. Their mutual desire. Again, she nodded. She could no more deny his needs than ignore her own.

Seemingly satisfied, he brought the foil packet to his mouth, and tore it open with his teeth. He pulled his lower body away enough for him to allow him to roll the condom onto his straining erection, then pointed himself at her hot opening. Instead of pushing forward as she *needed* him to, he paused for a moment, breathing deeply. She wriggled in an attempt to entice him forward but he stood his ground, looking down at her.

She couldn't wait. *Wouldn't* wait. With a growl, she grabbed his ass in her hands and pulled, impaling herself on his heated length until his balls slapped against her skin. Pleasure shot from her pussy to the ends of her limbs, hitting all the points in between. Her inner muscles clenched around him, and every nerve ending in her body buzzed as Ty's cock filled too-many-years' worth of emptiness deep, deep inside.

♫

The air left Ty's lungs in a whoosh, and spots danced before his eyes. His cock was buried to the hilt in Ashley's hot wet core, and for a moment he couldn't think of what was supposed to happen next. Then she started to squirm beneath him, and his body responded. He pulled his hips back, and thrust forward, even deeper than before. Her eyes fluttered shut, and her head fell back with a moan. Her pussy muscles clung to his cock, grasping him. He thrust into her, again and again, her cries urging him on. Pressure built in his body, focused on his cock. Ecstasy so intense it was almost painful.

Ashley's moans increased. Her hands gripped his hips, and she writhed, rubbing her wet clit against his groin. She wrapped her heels tight around his back, holding them together the way he loved. He angled her hips into the position that she most enjoyed. Without thought, they settled into the rhythms and movements each knew would please the other best.

When her hands fisted in his hair, he knew she was close. He flexed his hips back, then thrust so her hips left the dresser. Her nails raked down his back, and the pleasure-pain etched his skin, and shimmered along his veins. Her eyes flew open. He caught her gaze with his, and watched as her eyes widened, and her mouth formed the soundless "o" that always preceded her pleasure.

He loved seeing her like this, when her barriers crumbled, and she let her passion fly free. His thrusts quickened. He captured her mouth as she came, swallowing her cries with his lips. Her inner muscles milked his cock, triggering his own release. His hips pumped involuntarily, and his cock jerked as he emptied himself inside her.

Ashley collapsed against him, her head resting over his pounding heart. He wrapped his arms around her, and rested his chin on her head. He held her tight, unwilling to let feelings of intimacy between them slip away.

His breath bellowed in and out of his lungs. Her labored breath tickled the hairs on his chest. The muscles of her pussy twitched around him, aftershocks of her climax. Footsteps sounded in the hallway. Ashley jerked, and tensed beneath his hands like a rabbit preparing to flee.

There was a knock on the door. "Ty?" Luke called. "You in there?"

Ty turned to the door, but didn't let go of Ashley. He had to clear his throat before he could speak. "Yeah, I'm here. Just looking for my trunks."

"When you're done can you give me a hand with the keg?"

"Sure. Be out in a minute."

Luke's footsteps receded. Ashley pulled back, and Ty let her go. He reached down to remove the condom. She jumped off the dresser, scooped up her bathing suit bottoms, and tote, and dashed into the bathroom. Ty caught a glimpse of her naked ass before she pulled the door closed behind her. She was even sexier than he'd remembered.

The water came on, and Ty could hear soft movements as she did whatever women did in the bathroom after sex. His mouth widened into a grin. Maybe she would like some help. They could skip the party, and take a shower for two...

Ty pulled his jeans up, and smoothed down his hair, but the mirror over the dresser still reflected his *just-fucked* look. His smug, shit-kicking grin alone was a dead giveaway.

A few minutes passed. Ty shook his head in wry amusement. Some things never changed. Ashley was taking her own sweet time in the bathroom for a reason. She was stalling, postponing the moment when she'd have to face what had happened between them. She'd never been very good at confrontation.

But he could be patient. Hell, he'd waited three years – a few more minutes couldn't hurt. Not that it was easy, with her scent still on his body and the echo of her cries ringing in his ears. A performance like that warranted an encore – or three.

It hadn't always been this good, had it? He could never have survived her absence if this was what he'd been missing. But deep in his heart he knew the truth. Even while basking in the aftermath of their pleasure, his soul shuddered to recall how much he'd suffered when she'd gone. And the physical loss had been the least part of it.

Another few minutes passed. Ashley still hadn't reappeared, and no sound came from the bathroom. He stalked to the door, suspicion rising within him. He tried the doorknob, surprised when it turned.

The bathroom was empty, the door to the adjoining guest room open wide. He stepped through with a curse, knowing what he would find. The second room was empty too. Ashley was nowhere to be seen. A moment later he heard the unmistakable sound of a car starting. She'd run from him *again*.

Tension gripped his chest, but what bubbled up wasn't anger, but laughter. He threw his head back and let it out, not caring who heard him.

She couldn't be serious. After three years of silence, she shows up in town, fucks him like a wild animal, then runs out? Did she actually think that he would let her get away with that? That he would let her flee and not follow?

Not this time. This time she would learn the age-old lesson of the wild: running from a predator only makes them chase you. And the chasing makes the catching even better.

Chapter Eight

Ashley screeched to a halt behind Granny's house, jumped out of her car, and bolted for the front door. She dashed up the stairs, closed the door, and dove onto the bed. Only then did she allow herself to breathe.

I had sex with Ty Monroe.

She covered her face with her hands. Sex was too clinical a word for what they'd done, too sterile for the frantic clawing, grappling, thrust, and release they had shared. They'd *fucked* like animals, and it had been the most mind-blowing experience of her life.

She searched her conscience for the shock and regret she knew she should feel, but there was none, only a melting warmth and satisfaction that made her body tingle from head to foot. What was it about that man that made her lose her mind? She snorted – the list could go on for pages. Suffice to say that he was her weakness. Her poison. For Superman, it was Kryptonite. For Ashley Ford, Ty Monroe.

The worst part of it? Fucking Ty hadn't scratched the itch. No, it made her want to do it again. And again. And again. She groaned, and rolled onto her back. Regret prodded her at the thought of Rob. She'd bolted from Nashville to outrun her attraction to her singing partner, and what had she done? Jumped into bed with her ex. What the hell was wrong with her?

Men, that's what. Either one of those males was enough to make a woman crazy – two of them at the same time was definitely too much to handle, even if only in her thoughts.

Deep breath, Ashley. She needed to pull herself together. She was getting all worked up for nothing. So, she'd gotten a little carried away back at Val's–

A little? I fucked him half-clothed, and we hadn't even said two words to each other.

Another deep breath. Okay so she'd gotten a lot carried away. Three years of celibacy could do that to a woman. But it changed nothing. Ty was still the same man who had hurt her, the man she put behind her in order to pursue her dreams in Nashville. She would do well to remember that, and not get carried away again.

Nothing more would happen between them, that was all there was to it. She would be cool and polite to him when she saw him – *if* she saw him – and leave town tomorrow as she'd planned. She would not hide in this room until then. She would not hide her car in the garage behind the house. And no matter how tempted she was, she would not get in her car, and leave town a minute sooner than she'd planned

She tried more deep breathing to calm herself, but thoughts of her and Ty kept skittering through her brain. The feel of his body. The smell of his skin. The hard, hot thrust of his– She sat up and reached for her guitar. Few things could center or distract her better than music, and she really, *really* needed distracting right now.

She strummed a few chords, and her breathing slowed. She picked through one of Sweet Talk's older songs, and her heart rate returned to normal. She was about to start on a new piece that she and Rob were playing around with when Granny's voice carried up the stairs.

"Ashley, sweetheart?"

The bedroom was so small she could stick her head out the door, and look down the stairs without getting off the bed. "Yes, Granny?"

Granny stood by the door with a covered casserole dish in her hands. "I'm heading over to Amelia's to bring her some dinner." She held up the dish. "Poor dear had surgery on her hip, and is having trouble getting around."

Ashley nodded. "Tell her I say hello and to get well soon."

"I will, dear." The older woman gestured at the kitchen. "I left plenty of casserole in the oven. Chicken and cornbread. Bet you haven't had that in a long time."

Ashley smiled. It was her favorite. "None as good as yours Granny."

A low rumble sounded from down the road. A familiar sounding rumble. Ashley's smile faded, and she shook her head. It couldn't be. It *couldn't* be.

The sound got closer. It was.

Ty was here.

Ashley ducked back into the bedroom. Her car was around back so Ty might not realize she was home. Maybe he'd see Granny leaving and keep going. Granny wouldn't know to cover for her if he stopped. Hoping against hope, Ashley scooted over to the window, and lifted a corner of the curtain.

Ty pulled up in front of the house on his Harley and parked. He pulled off his helmet and laid it on the seat, but rather than turning towards the front door, his gaze went straight to her bedroom window. She dropped the curtain with a squeak, and fell back on the bed.

Firm footsteps sounded on the porch steps, and the screen door screeched open. Granny's voice carried from down the hall. "Well if it isn't Tyler Monroe. How are you doing, young man?"

"Very well, ma'am. And you?"

"I'm doing well too – better now that Ashley is home."

Ashley could picture him nodding to Granny, a triumphant light in his eyes. He cleared his throat. "If I'm not mistaken, Mrs. Ford, someone is about to get a delivery of your famous chicken and cornbread casserole."

Ashley heard her Granny chuckle, and could imagine the older woman waving a hand to dismiss the compliment. "Oh this. I made it special for Ashley, 'cause it's her favorite, but saved some extra for Amelia Dawson."

"Still feeling poorly since her surgery?"

"She is, but the fixing you did on her porch swing last week really cheered her up. That was kind of you."

"It was no trouble. Could I ask you a favor, Mrs. Ford – if there's anything else Mrs. Dawson needs, would you let me know? I know she's not the type to ask for help."

"No, she's not, but you can't blame her – don't no one like feeling like they need charity, even when they get to my age."

Ty made some comment that Ashley couldn't hear. Granny chuckled. "Oh Tyler, it's kind of you to say so."

Ashley shook her head with a reluctant smile. Ty could put

on the charm for women of all ages. He was like Rob in that way. Funny, she'd never thought of that before.

"I'd best be going, but if you're looking for Ashley, she'll be along in a moment." Ashley heard Granny put a foot on the bottom step. "Ashley, Tyler is here for you."

So much for escaping. "I'll be right down." She got up from the bed, and smoothed her T-shirt down over her shorts. Closing her eyes, she tried to recapture the calm she'd felt while playing the guitar, but all sense of tranquility had fled.

"Ashley?"

Granny wasn't going to leave until Ashley greeted her guest so she might as well get it over with. She paused at the door, trying to will the scarlet out of her cheeks. She'd screwed this man on a dresser at Val's house only an hour before, and now she had to speak to him in front of Granny. *Could this get any worse?*

Granny's voice drifted up the stairs again. "Tyler, I made plenty of casserole, so why don't you stay for dinner? I feel badly leaving Ashley alone when she's only going to be in town until tomorrow. I know she'd enjoy the company."

It got worse. Was Granny trying to give her a heart attack? Let him have a prior commitment, she begged silently, knowing that there was no way she'd get off that easily. Still, she held her breath.

"Why thank you for the invitation, Mrs. Ford. I couldn't possibly turn down an offer of your homemade casserole – and I'd be happy to keep Ashley company." Ashley could hear the satisfied smirk in his reply.

Unable to avoid it any longer, Ashley stepped into the hall, and started down the stairs. Ty came into view as she descended. Muscular legs and hips wrapped in crisp denim, a neat T-shirt stretched over his flat abs and strong chest, finally the strong jaw and dark hair. Hair she'd been pulling at not a half hour ago…

She stepped off the bottom step, and swallowed. "Ty."

He greeted her with a nod of his head. "Ashley."

Granny smiled. "I invited Tyler to join you for dinner. Didn't want you to have to eat alone."

He gave a modest shrug, but Ashley could see a smile playing around the corners of his mouth. He was enjoying this.

Ashley looked at Granny. "That's kind of you, but I don't mind waiting until you get back."

She patted Ashley on the arm. "I'll probably eat over at Amelia's, so you young folks should start without me. There's some salad in the fridge and peach cobbler for dessert."

"Your cobbler too? Mrs. Ford, you've made me a happy man."

Ashley wished she could feel the same. She struggled to keep a neutral expression on her face as her last hope for salvation gave her a hug, and turned towards the steps. Ty offered to carry Granny's dish to the car, and she handed it to him.

"Ashley honey," Granny called over her shoulder when she reached her car. "You take good care of Tyler, and enjoy your dinner."

"Thank you Granny. I will."

Ty turned towards Granny, but not before Ashley caught his smile. Granny's idea of taking good care of a man meant filling his belly, but Ashley knew that wasn't what Ty had in mind. She cursed the thrill that ran through her body at the thought, and stepped back into the hallway.

Granny drove off. When Ty's measured footsteps sounded

on the porch steps, Ashley panicked. Instead of heading into the kitchen as she'd intended, she dashed back upstairs. The screen door opened as she slipped through the bedroom door.

I just need a minute to pull myself together. She took a deep breath, and picked up the guitar from where she'd left it on the bed. She looked around for the case.

"I'll be right down," she called over her shoulder.

"No rush."

The words came from close behind her, and Ashley spun, almost losing her balance. Ty stood in the doorway of her tiny bedroom, one shoulder leaning against the frame. His body filled the narrow space, and his presence filled the room, reaching out to her. A masculine siren song she'd never been able to resist.

He pushed away from the doorframe, and Ashley's heart leapt into her throat. There wasn't much room to retreat, but she took a step backward, holding the guitar in front of her like a shield. Ty didn't come closer, as she'd expected. Instead he went over to the narrow twin bed, put one hand on it, and pushed down. His brow furrowed.

What was he doing?

He studied the mattress for a moment, then turned, and sat down hard. The bed responded with a loud screech. A wicked smile creased his face. "I'd forgotten how hard you have to bounce to make that sound. We never had any trouble hitting that note, did we Ashley?"

Heat raced up Ashley's neck and down her body, before pooling between her thighs. The guitar trembled in her hands. Ashley and Ty never had trouble getting time alone in the house when she'd lived here – and plenty of opportunities to make the bed screech. Now years later, Ty was in her bedroom again, between her and the door. But she'd vowed not to let him get to her again. With a deep breath, she put the guitar aside, and she said the first words that came to her mind.

"What do you want, Ty?"

Ty rested his elbows on his knees. He tilted his head as if considering her question, but the look on his face made her nervous. He leaned forward. "What do I want, Ashley? I want to know if you still make that mewling sound when I suck your nipples. If your cream still tastes like vanilla and burnt sugar. If you still pant and buck when I take you from behind."

Ashley's mouth dropped open. Her tongue slipped out to wet her lips.

His gaze fixed on hers, eyes narrowed. "I want to know how good it could be between us this time around. This afternoon gave me a taste, but it wasn't enough. I'm here for the rest." He nodded, and leaned back, a deceptively innocent expression on his face. "How about you – what do *you* want, Ashley?"

That list sounds pretty good to me. She kept that thought to herself.

His smile turned wicked. "You've always been impatient – though that scene at Val's must have set a new record. But I remember that you also liked to take it slow." He got up off the bed. "So how do you want it now, Ashley? Fast – or slow?"

He took a step toward her. She stepped back. He took another step forward, and she tried to become one with the closet door. A third step, and he was in front of her, his body an inch away, his face hovering above hers.

He filled the space before her, but she could step to the side if she wanted to. Could turn her head to avoid his kiss. It had always been like that, and they both knew it. He would send her body spinning out of control, emotions running wild, but never let her deny that it was what she wanted. Never let her pretend that she wasn't giving in to him by choice.

Damn him.

Ty's mouth descended slowly, but Ashley knew she couldn't back down now. He was right – this afternoon had only been a taste – and she was *starving*. Three years was too long to go without sex. Without satisfaction. Without the man who could give her both. She reached up to grab his shoulders, standing on tiptoe to close the distance between them–

And a car door slammed right outside.

Chapter Nine

Ashley jumped. Ty exhaled with a curse, and braced his hand against the closet door as footsteps sounded on the gravel path outside. Ashley took advantage of the reprieve, and scooted under his outstretched arm. But before she could escape, his hand shot out, and grasped her shoulder. She looked up into those wintry eyes.

"This isn't over, Ashley. You're not getting away this time."

He let go, and she stumbled back a step. *What did he mean, this time?* She shook off her confusion, and scrambled down the stairs. When she hit the first floor, she pushed the screen door open without thinking. It took her a moment to register who was walking towards her. Then her mouth dropped open. "Rob. What are you doing here?"

He took the porch steps two at a time. Ashley barely had enough time to note that he looked exceptionally delicious before he pulled her into a bear hug that lifted her off her feet. Her beasts crushed against his chest, and her already-sensitized nipples tightened into sharp peaks.

After a moment Rob put her down but didn't let go. If anything, his arms tightened around her until she was pressed against him from shoulder to thigh. His lips brushed her hair and he inhaled deeply. "Ash baby, I missed you."

His throaty whisper sent heat straight to her womb, and it took everything she had not to tilt her face to Rob's, and kiss him. That would be a bad idea – a *really* bad idea – but at the moment she was having a hell of a time remembering why.

Singing partner. Housemate. Best friend. Ty in her bedroom. She repeated those reasons like a mantra, but her libido didn't seem to be getting the message. Her hands itched to caress him, to fist in his hair... So much for her plan to cool off by putting some distance between them. It was ironic that she'd managed to control herself when Rob was in her bed, but was having trouble keeping her hands off him on Granny's porch. Was she ever going to be able to control herself around men again?

The screen door squeaked behind them, and Rob lifted his head. Ashley stepped back and he let one arm drop, but kept the other slung over her shoulders. A predatory look crept across his face. His shoulders straightened, and his chest expanded, while a muscle ticked in his jaw. She'd seen him adopt that look in photo shoots but never for real. It made him look dangerous – and *hot*.

She gathered her courage and turned to face Ty. His feet were planted slightly apart, arms hanging loosely at his sides. His face was expressionless, but his stance was one of a man poised on the edge of motion. He looked Rob up and down, eyes lingering on the hand that hung over her shoulder.

The moment stretched into tense silence. She knew she should say something, but words had fled. Her entire being was focused on the two sexy men sizing one another up on Granny's porch. They were a lot alike – under different circumstances, they might even be friends. In this situation, they were going to start marking territory if she didn't do something.

She stepped to the side, slipping out from beneath Rob's arm, and gestured at Ty. "Rob, you remember Ty Monroe, right? My..." *What – ex? Lover? Tormentor?* And what was Rob to her? *Best friend? Singing partner? Ongoing fantasy?*

Best to leave the labels out of it. She started over. "Rob, Ty Monroe. Ty, Rob Porter."

Rob stepped forward, Ty put his hand out, and the men shook. Their grip lasted a bit too long, and Ashley forced herself not to roll her eyes. It looked like she wasn't going to be able to avoid the pissing contest after all. She turned to Rob. "I didn't know you were coming, but you're just in time. Ty and I were about to sit down to dinner. Granny made some of her famous chicken and cornbread casserole."

She mentally kicked herself. Alone with the two men she lusted after, and she was playing the Southern hostess. On the other hand, having both of them here might save her from facing the questions and recriminations of either. At least for a little while.

Rob pulled his glare off of Ty, and turned her way. "I'd like that. I've been looking forward to seeing your Granny."

Ashley looked over her shoulder as she moved to the door. "I'm afraid she's not here right now – she's bringing dinner to a sick neighbor. But she'll be back soon. You are planning to stay, aren't you?"

"Yeah. I figured we'd caravan back to Nashville in the morning. We have a show tomorrow night."

As if she'd forget. She rolled her eyes, about to make a snide retort but Ty spoke first from behind her. "Opening for

We Were Angels at Bootleggers, right?"

Ashley looked at him in surprise. "Yeah."

"I hope there are still some tickets left."

Was he planning to come to see the show? Ashley felt something sweet and hopeful bubble up inside her. It deflated with his next comment. "After your performance at Charley's, I'm sure a lot of folks in Oak Valley are going to want to see you on the big stage."

Rob asked the question that Ashley couldn't. "And what about you? You coming to see us?" The way that he said *us* was like staking a claim.

Ty ran a gaze over her that felt as possessive as a brand, and gave Rob a feral smile. "Of course. Can't ever get me enough Ashley Ford."

True to her Southern roots, Ashley had tackled the awkward situation with food. The table groaned under casserole, salad, coleslaw and greens, with a pitcher of sweet tea to wash it down. Ty poured himself a glass, and looked at Rob Porter, the man who had interrupted his seduction of Ashley Ford three years earlier, and again just now. He shook his head. *Damned singer had lousy timing.*

Ashley passed something to Rob, and he said something Ty couldn't hear but made Ashley smile. She nodded, and Rob laughed. There was an ease between them, a closeness that made Ty's chest tighten. She'd fucked Ty, but Rob was the man she *lived* with. Worked with. Had left Ty to be with.

Ty's eyes narrowed. Had she and Rob slept together? He didn't think so, but could see from Ashley's demeanor that they were more than friends. So what did that make them? And what did it make Ty?

Ty looked more closely at the singer. How was it that he now found himself sitting across the table from Rob feeling a lot less hostile than expected?

He was tense, and certainly unsettled, but the anger he would have predicted in this situation was absent. Yeah, he was jealous of Ashley's relationship with Rob, and frustrated by the man's crappy timing, but on top of all that Ty was... intrigued. Something about this man pricked his curiosity. And seemed almost familiar. Maybe that's why Ty didn't feel as threatened as he should have, despite everything that pointed to Rob as a rival.

Was it because he'd seen Rob's face so often on Sweet Talk's album cover? No, it was more than that... The answer came to him, and he set his glass down. "Matt McKenzie."

Rob looked at him, the flash of confusion on his face giving way to suspicion. Ashley's forehead wrinkled in thought. "That name sounds familiar..."

Having figured out the mystery, Ty picked up his fork, and dug into the casserole. "We played football together in high school. He left before you moved here, Ashley, and his folks moved to North Carolina shortly after." He ate a bite, then gestured toward Rob. "That's who he reminds me of."

"Was he any good?" Rob's tone was casual but Ty could hear the wariness underneath, as if he were trying to decide if the comparison was a compliment or an insult.

"Best damned quarterback in the state. Got a scholarship to play ball at UT."

Recognition dawned in Ashley's face, and she laughed. "Now I remember that name – it was on the walls of every girls' bathroom in the school. He had quite a few female admirers."

And he wasn't interested in a single one of them. But few people knew that, and Ty wasn't about to share someone else's secrets. Interesting that Rob reminded him of the only man who had ever made him wonder... Ty shook his head. *Teenage curiosity, that's all it was.* No man had turned his head since Matt, so Ty was clearly in the hetero camp. And Rob was too, seeing how he was looking at Ashley. But then what was this familiar vibe that Ty was getting from him?

Rob leaned back, hooking an elbow over his chair. "Tell me more about this Matt guy. Good friend of yours?"

Had Ty imagined it or had there been an emphasis on the word "friend"? Like Rob knew something–no, that wasn't possible. Rob was probably making some slur about gays, implying that Ty and Matt were "fags." His estimation of the singer went down a notch.

"Yeah, we were friends. Matt was a good guy, and a damned good quarterback."

"He still play ball?"

Ty shook his head. "Busted his knee sophomore year, and decided to get a degree in business. Last I heard he was headed to Atlanta to work in a bank of some sort."

Ashley tilted her head. "I never heard that."

Ty shrugged. "Yeah, well, when he quit ball and his family left, folks 'round here stopped talking about him." Said good riddance more like it, when they heard rumors that he'd been caught in a compromising position with a physical therapist. One of the male ones.

Ashley nodded and turned back to her plate, but Rob continued to watch him. The singer had a laid-back thing going on, but Ty wasn't fooled – there was nothing lazy about the assessment going on behind those dark brown eyes.

After a moment, Rob nodded, as if to himself, and turned back to his plate. *What had the other man concluded?* It didn't matter. Ty shouldn't care. He reached for his glass, and washed his odd curiosity away with a gulp of Granny's sweet iced tea.

Chapter Ten

The rumble of a car approached the house, and cut off outside. Rob smiled. "No need for a doorbell 'round here – you can hear when anyone comes down that road."

Ty gave Ashley a sly sort of look. "We took advantage of that fact a couple of times, didn't we Ashley?"

Another reminder of her history with Ty. Rob could have kicked himself for bringing it up. Ashley blushed, and rose from her seat. With a quick *be right back* she went to the front door to see who had arrived.

Rob's gaze followed her through the kitchen door. When he turned back to the table, an icy blue gaze was pointed his way. He started to open his mouth to speak, but stopped. Sure, he had a million questions but few that he would ask Ty. He'd wait 'til he and Ashley were alone. Still he had to say something. "So you're still in Oak Valley. Ash told me you were sure to have left by now."

A corner of Ty's mouth quirked up in a smile. "Nice to know she thought of me." He shrugged. "I found a couple of things to keep me around."

Rob raised a brow, interested in spite of himself. "Like what?"

Ty's long fingers drew circles in the condensation on his glass. "I bought the local bar, Charley's. Ashley played there last night."

Rob nodded, trying to hide his surprise. Ty *owned* the bar where she'd played? She hadn't mentioned that. Rob wondered if she'd known. He schooled his tone to hide the depth of his curiosity. "Keeps you busy, eh?"

"At first, but not so much anymore – a business like that practically runs itself. Besides my real interest is in start-ups. Helping new businesses get off the ground." Ty's fingers stilled on the glass, and he pinned Rob with his pale gaze. "I'm attracted to challenges."

Just like that, the casual part of the conversation was over. Rob gave a sly smile of his own. "Are you really? So what kinds of challenges attract you the most?"

"The ones with the biggest payoffs."

Ty's words sent a shiver down Rob's spine, making him regret that the man across from him was a rival and not a potential lover. Yeah, Ty was his type all right, from his cool smile and icy gaze to his rock hard pecs and long, strong legs. And when he'd sized Ty up outside, Rob couldn't help noticing that he measured up in other significant ways too.

Rob looked away, rubbing a hand over his mouth. From their brief acquaintance three years ago, Rob didn't remember Ty being quite so *hot*. And now he'd come to Oak Valley to help Ashley fend off her ex, only to find himself attracted to the man. Rob shook his head. Complicated would be an understatement.

Ty lifted a brow in question, but Rob reached for his glass. There was no way he was going to share those thoughts.

The screen door slammed, and Ashley returned with a glass dish in her hands. "That was the neighbor returning a casserole dish Granny brought over last week. I swear she feeds half this town." She glanced between him and Ty, and her smile took on a forced stiffness – there was no way she could fail to notice the tension.

Her gaze fell to their empty plates. "I hope y'all left room 'cause Granny made peach cobbler."

Ty started to rise from his chair, but Rob jumped to his feet. "No need for you to get up Ty. I'll give Ashley a hand in the kitchen." *And have her to myself for a few minutes.* He stacked Ashley's plate on his, then requested Ty's with an open palm. The other man handed it over, his eyes narrowing as he looked from Rob to Ashley, and back again. Rob bit back a smirk.

He followed Ashley into the kitchen. As soon as they were through the doorway, and out of earshot he turned to her. "Ash, what the hell is going on?"

She turned away to put the dishes in the sink. "What do you mean?" The waver in her voice belied her innocent question.

He pointed towards the dining room. "Ash, that man broke your heart. Why are we having dinner with him like we're all old friends?'

"He stopped by right before you did, and Granny invited him. She's always liked Ty."

He shook his head in disbelief. "Liked him? Does she know what he did to you? How long it took you to recover after he tried to crush your dreams?"

Ashley shrugged. "Not really. I didn't share all the details with her."

"You didn't share." He let out an exasperated breath. "Well, I know the details, and I can't believe that even three years later that bastard has the nerve to keep sending you those looks."

"Looks? What looks?"

Rob huffed in exasperation – couldn't she see it? "Like he can't wait to get you back in his bed. As if you would after what he did."

Color washed from Ashley's neck to her hairline so quickly, it was like poured paint that ran up instead of down. He shook his head as an awful thought came to him. *That couldn't mean...?* "No way, Ash. No *fucking* way."

She looked away, but not before he caught the look of guilt on her face. An unidentifiable fury stormed through him; so fierce he had to clench his teeth to prevent himself from roaring out loud. She'd slept with him. Even after all Ty had done.

After she turned me down. He pushed that thought away, and put his hands on her shoulders, turning her to face him. "Please tell me I'm imagining things. Please tell me that you did *not* sleep with that man after being in town for less than forty-eight hours."

Ashley's eyes got big, then narrowed. "That's rich coming from you. How many men have you fucked on a few hours' acquaintance?" She shook her head. "Besides, weren't you the one who said I needed to get laid?"

What the hell? He whirled away, fighting to keep his anger in check, clenching his hands against his thighs. He took a few deep breaths. When he thought he could keep himself from going off on her, he turned back around. "I wasn't judging you for having sex, Ash. I— Have you forgotten what you were like after you left Oak Valley? After Ty broke your heart? Because I haven't. You were miserable. Barely functional." He shook his head. "Why would you want to do that to yourself again?"

Rob could see her lip quiver but she lifted her chin. "That's my business."

Her business? Sure – until he had to pick up the pieces. And weren't they a team? "What about Sweet Talk? With everything that's going on, everything riding on this next show... How could you jeopardize us like that?"

He regretted his words the moment they left his mouth, but she nodded. "I know. I know. It wasn't a good idea, but it's not like I planned it." She shrugged, and made a strange little laugh. "I... I couldn't help myself."

She had no trouble controlling herself around me.

He had to stop thinking that way. They were *friends*. Sure, he'd offered the other night, when she was laying in bed all soft and warm – he shook his head to get rid of the image, but it was replaced by a vision of Ty's body wedged between Ashley's thighs, cock pounding deep into her.

Jealousy gripped Rob's gut at the same time that his balls tightened with lust. Neither of those reactions were useful in this situation so he ignored them in favor of the growing urge to plant a fist in the blue-eyed face he'd been admiring across the table. He closed his eyes. Good thing they were in different rooms, otherwise Rob wasn't sure that even his momma's raising would have been enough to keep him from doing something really stupid.

"Rob? You okay?"

He opened his eyes. Ashley was looking at him with a woeful expression. She put her hands on his arm, as if she knew what he was itching to do. "I'm sorry, Rob. It probably wasn't the smartest thing to do but it's too late now. I'll just have to deal with the consequences." She shrugged but Rob saw the sheen of tears in her eyes.

Rob let out a breath, forcing himself to relax, and opened his arms. With a look of relief, Ashley stepped into them, and laid her head against his chest. He could feel her heart going a million miles a second. Or was that his? They were both on the edge, body tense, emotions running wild. All because of the man sitting at Granny's table.

Rob didn't know how he managed to get through the rest of the meal with that man but one thing was clear. He was not going to let Ty get between him and Ashley again.

The Bootleggers show was about to start. Ashley's high-heeled boots clicked on the worn linoleum backstage. Piped-in music filled the club, and she could hear the buzz of the crowd pumped up by a DJ from Nashville's most popular country station. Wringing her hands like a Southern belle from an old film, she fixed her gaze on the floor in front of her, and paced. Back and forth. Back and forth. Click. Click. Click.

She heard footsteps, and looked up when Rob stepped in front of her. She stopped short to avoid a collision, but couldn't look him in the eye. They hadn't spoken about Ty since Rob had confronted her in the kitchen yesterday, but Ashley couldn't shake the feeling that she'd let him down in some way. And now they were about to go onstage.

Rob put his hands on her shoulders, and she flinched. He shook his head. "Calm down Ash. You're gonna be great."

Of course he would say that. "But what if I'm not? What if I suck?" She didn't say *again*. She didn't have to. They both knew how flat she'd been at the studio the other day. She'd done okay in her second set at Charley's, but that could have been a fluke.

Rob shook her shoulders, and she raised her gaze to his face. His eyes were narrowed, and his expression uncharacteristically stern. "You listen to me. Ashley Ford never sucks. *Never.*" His frown softened into a smile.

She nodded and tried to smile back at him, but her face wouldn't cooperate. With a sigh he pulled her close, and held her head to his chest. A shiver raced through her body, and her belly clenched in pleasure. A different kind of tension started to build.

His voice resonated under her ear. "Ash, you've had ups and downs but even on your worst day, you're amazing. Maybe not as good as *you* want it to be but still really, really talented."

She nodded, her cheek rubbing against his chest like a cat's. "Okay, but–"

He pulled back, and looked at her. "No buts. You told me you played well at Charley's the other night – do what you did then and you'll be awesome."

Ashley shook her head, and Rob put up a warning finger, but she couldn't bite back the objections that sprang to her lips. "That was a tiny bar, Rob. This is a *concert*." She pointed to the curtains that blocked the audience from view. "There are hundreds of people out there."

"Yeah so what?" He nodded. "You know what you need?"

Her mind jumped to what he'd said in her bed, about needing to get laid. Was he offering again? It was on the tip of her tongue to ask, when he stepped back so suddenly that she stumbled forward. Without a word he spun her so that her back was to his front. His hands rested once again on her shoulders, while his thumbs dug into to the tight muscles on the sides of her neck.

She smiled. They'd developed a backrub ritual during their early shows when she'd been terrified of going on stage. She hadn't needed it for a while, but damn did it feel good. Too good. She tried to relax, but her core muscles clenched at his touch, and a shock of desire raced through her when the back of his hand brushed the shell of her ear. The nape of her neck. Were his fingers roaming more than usual? Her earlier anxiety faded, replaced by arousal. Her nipples tightened into peaks.

*Oh God, I can't go onstage like thi*s.

Rob kneaded her muscles. "You're a born performer, Ashley. A natural, whether you're in front of a dozen people or a thousand. That hasn't changed."

His breath caressed her nape as he spoke, and she shivered. She cleared her throat, and stepped out from under his hands, crossing her arms to hide her physical reaction.

Rob smiled, seemingly oblivious to her predicament. "Ash, you were hot in front of your hometown crowd, right? And some of those folks are going to be here tonight?"

She nodded, not sure where he was going with this.

"Ok, then play for *them*. Forget about the rest of the crowd – you can't see them beyond the stage lights anyway. Focus on your friends. Play like you're in a little country bar." He tilted his head. "I hear that's what Jennifer Nettles does when she's nervous."

For a moment she forgot her arousal, and peered at him, eyes narrowed. Jennifer Nettles was one of her idols. "Really?"

Rob nodded. "True. I heard it on WNIX. Or maybe it was in the *Music City Weekly*."

She laughed and shook her head. "Sure, Rob."

"Well, it got you to laugh, which was the point."

A young guy with shaggy hair and a walkie-talkie poked his head around the curtain. "Um, Mr. Porter. You wanted to ask the lighting guy something?"

Rob nodded. "That's right. I'll be right back. Try to relax." He gave her a kiss on the top of the head, and followed Walkie-

Talkie Guy down the hall.

She took a deep breath, and wiped her hands on her jeans. Maybe Rob was right – she had played well at Charley's the other night. Come to think of it, she did feel a little better than she had during the practice session. More energetic. More *alive*.

And more aroused. Now that Rob was gone her body was calming down, but she wasn't entirely back to normal. She took a deep breath, and raised her hand, stopping herself before she ran it through her hair. The stylist had spent a half-hour fixing it – she'd best not mess it up.

Ashley turned at the sound of someone stepping into the room. A young woman with a ponytail held a clipboard, looking nervous. "Um, Miss Ford, there's someone here to see you. Said you'd be expecting him...?"

The girl's voice trailed off, and Ty stepped up beside her.

Ashley's mouth went dry, and the arousal she'd been trying to forget flooded her like a tsunami. A black button-down hugged his chest, tucked into black jeans that skimmed his muscular legs. Ashley had a memory of the hair on those long legs tickling her inner thighs the other day– She swallowed, and crossed her arms. "Ty? What are you doing here?"

A panicked look crossed the girl's face. She looked from Ashley to Ty, and back. "Oh no, was he not supposed to be here? I'm so sorry, I..."

Ty raised a hand to cut off the girl's apology. "It's okay, Lorilee. You did fine. I wanted to surprise Miss Ford before the show. Wish her good luck. "

The girl breathed out a sigh of relief, and nodded, as if this explained everything. Ty put a hand on Lorilee's shoulder, and the girl turned to him with an expression that bordered on adoration.

"Why don't you grab some water for Miss Ford?" He gestured at the table behind them, which already held a half-dozen full bottles. "I think we're running a little low."

The girl blushed, and turned to Ashley. "I'll do that, Miss Ford," she said, as if it had been Ashley's request, and scampered off.

Ashley watched her go, then turned back to Ty, shaking her head. "Not easy to get backstage without a pass. Charmed your way in, eh?" Not that she was surprised. The man had a way about him that said that he belonged anywhere he chose to be.

He shrugged. "Act like you belong, and people believe you. I wanted to see you before the show. To wish you luck. Not that you need it. You sounded great Friday night."

The compliment warmed her, but she shook her head, and repeated what she'd said to Rob. "Nothing personal, but Charley's is a country bar in the middle of nowhere. This is a concert hall."

"I wasn't referring to Friday. The crowd at your usual place loves you, and your opening for the Hounds last year was fantastic."

Ashley's jaw dropped. "But… How would you know?"

"I was there. And I've gone to other shows."

"What? Since when?" Her question was a barely a whisper.

"Since you left."

The music changed to the song that came before their entrance, but Ashley could hardly hear it. Her mind raced to make sense of what his words. Three years ago, Ty had tried to discourage her from joining Rob's band. *So why had he followed her career since then?*

The question was still ringing through her head when Ty stepped close – so close she could feel the warmth of his breath on her face. Before she could think, his hand came up to her jaw, and his mouth came down. His lips were warm and firm, and when she gasped, his tongue slipped in her mouth. Heat coursed through her for the second time that evening, and again her nipples tingled.

After a moment or ten – Ashley couldn't say – he started to pull away. Not wanting the kiss to end, she leaned forward, and he nibbled her lower lip. His hand stroked her jaw. "For luck," he said, stepping back. She hadn't realized that she'd raised her hands to his arms until they dropped away. Ty wiped the back of his hand across his mouth, and it came away with smudges of red lipstick, which she'd put on thick for the show.

"Lorilee," he called over his shoulder. The girl reappeared. "Miss Ford is going to need some help freshening up her make-up." The stage girl nodded and bolted off as if she'd been given an order.

Ty gave Ashley a long stare, then turned and left without another word.

Lorilee returned with the make-up case and an unnecessary bottle of water. Ashley took out a tube of scarlet lipstick, and stared in the mirror. The song that preceded their act came to an end. Ashley shook her head to clear it and swirled the color across her mouth. She straightened her shoulders and turned towards the stage.

Rob stood by the curtain. He nodded towards the stage. "Show time, beautiful."

How long had he been standing there? Had he seen Ty kiss her?

The voice of the DJ boomed through the speakers. "And now country fans, put your hands together, and give a warm welcome to Nashville's one and only Sweet Talk!"

Chapter Eleven

Ashley bolted past like a thoroughbred from the gate. Rob jogged to catch up, coming alongside her as they burst onto the stage. The whole show went like that – Ashley set the pace, and he followed, soaking up the pure joy of her performance. Whatever had been holding her back was gone now. She sounded stronger, and more powerful than ever.

Hot damn. Ashley had never been a mellow performer, but tonight she went beyond her usual energy. When they launched into their first semi-hit "Cherry Pie", and Ashley sang the line *I got a little something sweet for you*, the audience went insane. More than a few of the guys in the front looked like they were in love.

She was on fire. Ecstatic. She made love to the audience with her voice and her guitar, and they loved her right back, screaming and calling her name. Being onstage with her was incredible – feeling her energy, and watching her body move and sway with the music.

And a huge turn-on, too. Rob couldn't stop touching her. His hands were drawn to her body like iron filings to a magnet. Sparks jumped between them with each contact. His fingers at the small of her back, his arm brushing her hip. They'd always been good together, but tonight, their chemistry was explosive. It wasn't only musical – it was *sexual*.

This was the woman who'd been worried about her performance? He wished they'd invited scouts to this show. They'd land a recording deal in a heartbeat. She hadn't regained her former passion – she'd surpassed it into realms Rob had only suspected she could achieve.

What had changed? Where had this new energy and enthusiasm come from? Was it the new venue? The break from Nashville? Being home again? Rob threw her a glance. He had another suspicion…

He danced around Ashley, scanning the audience. Most of the faces beyond the stage lights were a blur but still he looked for one in particular – there. In the balcony. Ty sat with Val and a few others in the VIP seats.

That's where Ashley's gaze kept returning, the face she focused on as she sang. Sure Rob had told her to sing to her friends, but he hadn't meant that she should focus on Ty. Worse, she was *singing* to him, like a fucking serenade. Jealousy hit Rob like a sucker-punch to the gut. He fought to keep a scowl off his face. Was that the reason energy crackled off her like a live wire? Had sex with Ty released her inner passion, the kiss Rob had witnessed backstage made her come back to life? The joy Rob had felt moments ago morphed into dark green envy.

Fucking Ty. Who the hell was he, coming back into Ashley's life now? Nothing had changed. No matter how attractive he was, Ty was still the same bastard who had tried to *crush* Ashley's dreams. Dreams that Rob had made come true.

One more number. Rob forced himself to keep smiling. Ashley introduced their new song, a love song that they'd completed a few weeks ago. She'd wanted to try it out in front of a smaller audience at their usual bar, but Rob had insisted on debuting it at a bigger venue. She started singing, and Rob stepped up beside her, sliding an arm around her waist. She reciprocated, and they sang the first verse arm-in-arm. Rob could feel her voice resonating in her chest. Her body was hot. Her breasts, warm and heavy, pressed against his side.

He glanced over at Ashley - her gaze was locked on Ty. Was she singing the fucking song to him, the one she and Rob had written together? *Hell no.* He and Ash were a team. Meant to be together. She might have fucked Ty, but she was still Rob's partner, and he'd be damned if he'd give her up without a fight.

They sang the last words. Rob pulled Ashley around to face him, then dipped her as if they were dancing. Surprise flashed across her face followed by a desire that made Rob freeze in shock – but only for a moment. Then his mouth came down on hers. There was a split second hesitation, then Ashley wrapped her arms around him, pulling their bodies together. Her tongue brushed his lips, and twin shocks of lust and surprise rocked him. The kiss turned into a full-on, passionate, take-no-prisoners embrace that made his cock come to attention. This wasn't for the audience – she was responding to *him*.

Brad was waiting for them backstage. "You guys rocked. The crowd loved you. And that chemistry." He shook his hand like he'd burned his fingers. "Smoking. The DJs are going to be talking about this for weeks." He smiled. "Ashley Ford is back."

Ashley was flying, her mind spinning, and her body on fire after a half hour on stage. And then that kiss. What the hell had that been about? She'd fantasized about Rob for weeks, but nothing had prepared her for the way her body would cleave to his when they touched. *Damn.*

She shot a glance Rob's way, but he was talking to a DJ. Someone handed her a water bottle. She gulped it down. Another someone started speaking to her but the words drifted past. She smiled and nodded at what seemed like the right places. Her lips were moving – from the look on the other person's face the right words were coming out. More congrats. Slaps on the back for Rob, hugs and kisses for her.

Rob looped an arm over her shoulders. Her every nerve went on alert. He pulled her close. "Ashley's pretty amazing, but even she needs a rest after a performance like that."

Brad got the hint, and turned to the group clustered around them. "Okay, folks, let's not crowd our stars. They need a chance to recover." He gave them a wink.

She wound her way through the maze of curtains and doors, glad for Rob's hand on her back. In her current state she wasn't sure she could navigate the way herself. Brad talked the whole way about possible gigs, interviews, and other appearances. His hands flew as he spoke.

All because of that kiss. No, it was more than that. There had been a whole new chemistry between them. A connection she'd never felt before. Music and passion fueled by desire. The weeks of arousal she'd felt around him had culminated in the magic they'd shared onstage. *But where had it come from? And why had he kissed her?*

Rob escorted her through the dressing room door. After a few more questions and promises to set up interviews, the last of the well-wishers left the room. They were alone. She closed the door, pausing for a moment before she turned to face Rob.

His face was hidden as he pulled his damp t-shirt over

his head. Sweat pasted his hair to his skin, and made his chest gleam. Ashley's gut tightened, and she licked her lips, looking away to calm the lust that made her feel like her skin was stretched too tight.

She caught her reflection in the mirror. Her eyes were bright and her cheeks flushed. Her lips were swollen and her lipstick smeared – the same lipstick that she'd transferred to Ty's lips, and was now smudged across Rob's. She'd kissed two men tonight. Her inner muscles clenched, and she felt moisture drip onto her panties. It wasn't sweat.

She lifted her gaze to Rob's reflection. Behind her he stretched, making the muscles of his back ripple, and her throat went dry. Was this what happened when she broke her three-year drought – she wanted sex with every man in sight? Of course, Rob wasn't "every man." He was one of the most important people in her life, and someone she should not be lusting after, although she was having serious trouble remembering why.

Then there was Ty. Beautiful serious Ty, who'd been in the audience more times than she realized, and out there again tonight. How could she reconcile the horrible way things had ended between them with what was happening now? She buried her head in her hands. She'd been staring at Ty when Rob grabbed her around the waist, and kissed her.

Ty, Rob – both men made her so hot she couldn't think straight. What was wrong with her that she couldn't figure out what – or who – she really wanted?

That's not true, said a voice deep within. She shushed it fast. What that voice wanted wasn't possible. Wasn't the kind of thing nice girls thought about.

Who said you're a nice girl?

She looked into the mirror in surprise and shoved *that*

thought back into the dark corner where it belonged.

She lifted her hair off her neck to cool off. Rob tossed his sweaty tee shirt onto the couch. With his gaze locked on hers in the mirror, he stalked towards her, stopping right behind her. His hot chest was a hairsbreadth away, and the heat of his body sank into her skin. She wanted so badly to take that one step back that would bring her body into contact with his.

But it would change everything. She couldn't bring herself to do it – even after that kiss.

His hands came up to her shoulders to massage her like he had a hundred times before. But he had no shirt on, and her body was still on fire. She shuddered, hoping that he would chalk it up to residual adrenaline.

He gave her a feral grin in the mirror. "We were hot tonight, Ash. *Damn* hot. We've been good before, but tonight was something else. We were *great*." His hands skimmed down her arms to her hips, and his lips nuzzled her ear. Ashley stiffened with shock and arousal. Gooseflesh rose on her arms. He continued. "You were amazing, Ash. There was *fire* in you. A passion I've never seen. It was incredible," his voice dropped, "and *so fucking hot*."

Those last words were spoken against her jawbone, his lips were so close to hers. All she had to do was turn her head and his mouth would meet hers again–

A sharp knock made her jump. Another interruption. She should probably be grateful.

Lorilee's voice came through the door. "Miss Ford?"

Ashley cleared her throat. "Yes, Lorilee."

"There's someone here to–"

The dressing room door opened before the other woman could finish speaking. Ty stood there, looking like he owned the place. He scanned the room, taking in every detail of the scene. His gaze dropped to where Rob's hands branded her body. Ashley stepped forward. Rob's fingers tightened on her hips but she slipped out of his grasp.

Lorilee looked back and forth between Ashley and Rob, concern growing on her face. "He said he had business with you backstage..."

"It's okay, Lorilee," Ashley said for the second time tonight. She couldn't see Rob nor interpret the look on Ty's face. The sooner the other girl left, the better.

"Good. Great. Let me know if you need anything else." Lorilee slipped behind Ty, and disappeared.

Ty stepped into the room, and closed the door behind him. His eyes glittered with an odd sort of light, but his features held no expression. It reminded Ashley of the time he'd tried to teach her poker. She'd mastered the rules easily enough, but had never managed to beat him because of the damned poker face he wore now.

A tense silence filled the room, broken only by Rob's breathing and the hammer of Ashley's heart. Rob shifted behind her. In the reflection she saw that his stance was loose, but even from a few paces away she could feel the tension strumming through his body.

Rob broke the silence. "So, how'd you like the show?" The words were simple enough but Rob's tone made them into more of a taunt than a question.

"You guys were great." The admiration in Ty's voice was real, and Ashley thought she felt Rob relax a fraction.

"The crowd couldn't get enough of Ashley, could they?"

Ty shook his head. "Can't say I blame them."

Rob chuckled, but it wasn't a happy sound. "I guess some

people are smart enough not to let true talent slip through their fingers."

What the hell was going on? Aside from his joking proposition the other night, Rob had never indicated that he wanted her - so why the possessiveness? Was he just looking out for his professional interests? Could this be his idea of protecting her from Ty?

A tightening of Ty's jaw was the only indication that Rob's words hit their mark. He swallowed, then looked at Ashley. His expression softened. "You were wonderful."

"Thanks." Her throat was so dry it came out like a whisper.

Rob's fingers brushed her lower back, and she shivered. "She was better than that - she was *hot*."

The last word was a soft gasp that made Ashley's skin tingle. She turned away to hide her reaction, but couldn't resist peeking at Ty from the corner of her eye. His smile was a secret sly kind of thing, and he caught her gaze as he nodded. "*Scorching*. Even hotter than I remembered."

Ashley sucked in a breath as her face flamed. Ty wasn't talking about the show anymore. The hand against her back clenched into a fist. Rob had caught Ty's meaning too.

Okay, it was time to put a stop to the testosterone display before... Before what, Ashley couldn't say. She shifted her weight, ready to put some distance between herself and both men. But before she could move, Ty was right in front of her. Startled, she took a stumbling step backwards, and bumped into Rob. His erection pressed into her ass.

She started to pull away but Rob's hands grasped her hips. His heat cradled her back. Ty's breath fanned her face. The arousal that had been smoldering within her leapt into flame. Her body clenched. Nipples tightened into hard points. Ty raised his hand to her jaw, and brought his mouth to hers. His tongue thrust between her lips. She stiffened, expecting Rob to protest, so she was completely unprepared when he rubbed against her, and nipped the outer shell of her ear.

Oh God. They were treating her like the rope in a game of sexual tug-of-war – so why was she so turned on?

A knock sounded on the door, and Ty froze. Rob stepped back an inch, but she could still hear his labored breathing. She exhaled with a silent curse. Another interrupted seduction – the third in as many days. She didn't know whether to be pissed or relieved.

Ty rested his forehead against hers. "Val brought a few friends from home to see the show, and they want to know if they can come back and party with the stars. I told them I'd ask but I guess they got impatient."

Rob snorted behind her as Val's voice carried through the door. "Hey Ash – can we come in?"

"One sec!" Ashley slipped out from between them, and turned to the mirror avoiding their eyes in the reflection. "Come on in," she said, smoothing down her hair.

Rob was pulling on a tee shirt as Val opened the door, and poked her head in. In the hall behind Val, Ashley could see some of folks who had been at the barbecue. Her friend made a quick survey of the scene, then her gaze landed on Ashley. Ashley gave a weak smile, praying that she could come up with a plausible story before her friend grilled her, because there was no way she was going to tell Val what really happened. Especially when she had no idea herself.

Val nodded, then opened her arms wide, and gave her Beatles-worthy shriek. Both Rob and Ty winced. Ignoring them, Val pushed into the room, and wrapped Ashley in a hug.

"Oh my God, girl. You were unbelievable. I've seen you play before but never – *never* – like that. You were on fire."

And that kiss." Keeping an arm around Ashley's shoulders, she turned to Rob. "Boy, that was some hot stuff out there. I don't know if you guys planned that or not but it knocked the audience on their asses. The chemistry between you two – *ooweee*. I swear I thought people were going to start getting it on right there in the audience, you were making 'em so hot!"

Val turned towards Ty with a gleam in her eye. Ashley tried to pull away, but Val held her close, her arm a vice around Ashley's shoulders. "Ain't that right, Ty?"

Ty smiled. "Wouldn't dream of arguing with you, Val."

Val nodded with satisfaction. "Smart man." She looked at Ashley and Rob. "So what do y'all say about a little *par-tay* in honor of the hottest country duo in Nashville? You guys must know a million bars around here."

Ashley spoke. "Don't you guys want to see the rest of the show? We're just the opening act."

Val dismissed the idea with a wave of her hand. "We came to see you guys. As far as we're concerned, the best part of the show is over. So where to?"

Ashley felt warmth spread through her chest at Val's words. Damn, it was good to have her friend here.

"There aren't so many of y'all, so we could go back to our place," Rob said. Ashley noticed that he looked at Ty as he spoke. Rob seemed to be making some sort of point. Emphasizing that he and Ashley lived together?

Val smiled. "Great. We can pick up some booze on the way and if I know Ashley, you've got a pizza place on speed dial." She put her hands on her hips and looked at Rob sternly. "Unless that's not fancy enough for you Nashville types."

Rob laughed. "That would be my dinner every night if Ash didn't make me cook once in a while."

"Then what are we waiting for?"

The small group from the dressing room quickly morphed into a full-blown party. Some backstage folks joined them, and Rob called a few friends, so now thirty-plus people crowded their small living room, eating pizza, drinking beer, and shouting happily over the music. Jealousy flared in Ashley when Kyle, one of Rob's past hook-ups, arrived. She was being ridiculous of course. That onstage kiss had been a gimmick for the audience, nothing else. Besides, she'd had sex with Ty – why shouldn't Rob have some fun with an old lover too?

Fun with Kyle didn't seem to be in Rob's plans. Instead, he kept brushing up against Ashley. Flirting with her. Touching her. They'd always been affectionate, but this was different. It seemed more... intimate somehow. The fact that he threw a glance at Ty each time didn't escape Ashley's notice, either.

Ty was no better. His fingers lingered on her arm when he spoke to her, his hand brushed her hip when he walked by. And of course, his gaze sought Rob's each time.

Whatever game the men were playing, it was driving Ashley crazy. And turning her on. Her skin was hypersensitive, every nerve ending alive. A half hour into the party she'd had to change her panties, and now she crossed her arms over her chest to hide her nipples, which were so erect they hurt. She'd never been so aroused in her life.

By the time the party wound down Ashley felt as if she'd had hours of foreplay. One touch and she'd come. From the looks that Rob and Ty had been giving her all night, they had more than one touch in mind. Both of them. What the hell was she going to do?

The apartment slowly emptied until only Ashley, Val, and the two men remained. She and Val made a sweep of the room, gathering beer bottles, and putting the empties in a box. Rob was putting away the guitar he'd been strumming. When Ty stepped out of the room, Val leaned in close. "So what now?"

Ashley pretended ignorance. "Huh? What do you mean?"

"Ashley, those two boys have been eying you all night like hungry lions over a gazelle." Val nudged her with an elbow. "Think it will come to blows?"

Ashley glanced over her shoulder. Rob was fiddling with something over by the couch, and Ty stacked empty pizza boxes on the kitchen counter. Both men seemed tense. So was she. She shook her head. "I don't think so. I mean, I hope not..."

Val laughed, picked up the box of bottles, and headed to the door. Ashley followed. "So what are you going to do?" Val asked in a whisper.

"I don't know."

Val rolled her eyes. "What do you *want* to do?"

What did she want? She didn't know. Or was it that she couldn't admit it?

Val nodded at the door. Ashley opened it, and Val stepped past her into the hallway. Ashley followed.

"You sure you can carry that?" Ashley asked. Maybe if she could get away from the apartment for a few minutes she'd be able to think clearly.

Val saw through her, of course. "Your place is here. So what are you going to do?"

Ashley *shh'ed* her friend with a wave of her hand, and pulled the door closed behind her. "I don't know. I can't choose between them."

Val gave her a wicked smile. "Then don't." Ashley's mouth

dropped open but Val was already heading down the hall humming the love song they'd performed before Rob's kiss.

Ashley took a deep breath, and leaned back against the wall. The two men who had filled her life and her fantasies for as long as she could recall were waiting for her behind this door.

Chapter Twelve

Ashley slipped back into the apartment. She'd hardly made a sound, but both men turned to look at her. The sexual tension snapped into place like a plucked guitar string.

What was she going to do now?

What she'd said to Val was true – she couldn't choose between them. She'd fantasized about Rob for so long, and the fact that he returned her interest made her giddy with desire. At the same time, her body burned for Ty with a flame that had never gone out, only gotten brighter now that she'd been in his arms again.

She let out a slow breath. It was too much to think about now. Maybe she should go to bed, and sort out her feelings some other time.

There was another option…

The voice in her head sounded a lot like Val's. She quickly hushed it. Maybe a drink would calm her down. She'd been too wired from the show, and too edgy with arousal, to do more than nurse one beer.

Feigning a calm she didn't feel, she started across the room to the coffee table, where a few unopened beers stood. She was halfway there when Ty caught her eye. The desire in his gaze froze her in place. He stalked toward her, his eyes glittering like a cat that liked to play with its food before devouring it.

A hand landed on her hip from behind, and she jumped. Rob's body wasn't touching hers but was close enough that she could feel his heat against her back.

It was a replay of the scene in the dressing room. Rob behind her. Ty in front. No one spoke but anticipation hung in the air – they were waiting for her to make a move. To decide what – and who – she wanted.

The moment had come to choose or walk away. *Or propose something else. Something insane.*

Would the men go for it? Would two alpha males be willing to share?

Ashley swallowed, and placed her hand on Ty's chest. His heart pounded against her fingers. A victorious smile curved Ty's mouth, and Rob's fingers slid off her hip. Before she could lose her courage, she took a step backward, pressing against Rob. She heard a soft gasp, and his hands came up to her hips again, and his cock pressed against her backside. Ty's smile faded.

A hollow feeling filled Ashley's gut. Had she made a horrible mistake?

Ty looked at her. Then his gaze flicked over her shoulder to where Rob was standing. She held her breath.

Ty's gaze returned her face, eyes burning with desire. A wave of desire swept through her, making her knees weak.

Ty lifted his hand to her face. The backs of his knuckles brushed her cheek. With one finger he traced her lips, then drew a path along her jaw and down her neck. It dipped into her cleavage, and her heart raced. With his gaze still fixed on hers, he tugged on her shirt until the top button slipped free. Pink satin and lace peeked out of the gap.

Rob's hands moved up under her shirt to her waist. His thumbs rubbed soft circles against her skin. His hands slid up her body until his fingers brushed the undersides of her breasts. Ty's gaze flicked down to where Rob's hands touched her, and his nostrils flared. Rob raised his hands to cup her breasts and, although she couldn't see his face, she knew that he was watching Ty as he did it. Rob thumbs brushed her nipples, and she whimpered. His growl of triumph rumbled in her ear.

A flare of desire lit Ty's eyes. Ty grabbed her hips, and crushed his mouth to hers. His tongue thrust between her lips, as his cock pressed against her. Rob's cock rocked against her ass. A shudder rocked her body and she moaned. She was sandwiched between two men. Four hands touched her, two mouths kissed her skin. Two solid bodies, two rock hard cocks. All for her pleasure.

When she was light-headed with desire, Ty's lips left hers, and he leaned back to look in her face. Rob's hands stilled on her breasts, and he turned her so that she could see both of them. "You okay, Ash?" he asked softly.

She knew that he was really asking – was she okay with what they were doing? All three of them? She was. She really, *really* was, and wanted more. She nodded.

Ty tilted his head, and Ashley knew what was coming next. He wouldn't be content with knowing she was okay. He'd want more. "Is this what you want, Ashley?" he asked. "Both of us to touch you like this? Together?"

She took a deep breath, and closed her eyes. It was easy to lead them in this dance, but Ty wanted her to acknowledge what they were doing. To ask for what she wanted. She took a deep breath, and closed her eyes. She craved these men, and wanted them both at the same time, but could she admit it out loud?

Yes. She was too aroused to turn back. Too far gone to stop now, and not regret it for the rest of her life. She opened her eyes, and nodded. But, that wasn't enough – she owed them better. She nodded. "Yes, I want both of you. Now."

The restraints came off. If she thought the men were passionate before, it was nothing compared to what her words unleashed. Rob pulled her back against him, grinding his cock against her ass, and kneading her breasts in his palms. Ty's mouth came down on hers in a kiss that was as rough as it was exciting. He reached for the buttons of her shirt. Rob's hands left her breasts to give the other man access, and he cupped her jaw, gently turning her head, so they could kiss. His tongue delved into her mouth. Ty removed her shirt and bra, and leaned forward to circle her nipples with his tongue. One breast, then the other. The pleasure that shot through her was so powerful that her knees gave way. She would have fallen if the two men hadn't been there to catch her.

She may have initiated this, but now the men were in charge. Rob held her against his body, and backed the two of them to the couch. He lowered her gently onto the cushions, then settled next to her. Ty sat on her other side. Both men reached for her at the same time. Ty's long elegant fingers lifted one breast. Rob's rough hand cupped the other. This time Ty nuzzled her ear while Rob leaned forward to lave and suck her nipples.

Rob's hands slid over her hip to rest on her thigh. Ashley whimpered, and her pussy muscles twitched at the almost-but-not-close-enough contact. She was wet and aching inside for a touch – *any* touch. With two cocks, two tongues, and four hands, she shouldn't have to wait long.

Rob must have read her mind. He knelt before her, and started to undo her jeans. Ty's hand dove into her panties before her jeans were even fully open, and cupped her damp mound. His finger pressed her clit, and she nearly shot to the ceiling.

Ty slipped one finger inside her wet slit, and started pumping it slowly. She writhed against him. "More," she gasped, and he complied, spreading her wider with a second finger. She pressed against him, wanting to feel him deeper inside.

Rob pulled her jeans down her legs, and added them to the discard pile. Somehow he managed to take her panties and socks with them. He knelt between her legs, his gaze fixed on her pussy. He licked his lips.

What was he thinking as he watched Ty's fingers pump in and out? If the expression in his dark eyes was anything to go by, it was turning him on. Ty angled his arm out. His fingers were still inside her, but his hand no longer pressed against her clit. She missed that pressure, and wriggled her hips, trying to find it again. Instead she nearly levitated off the couch when a warm, wet tongue lapped her from slit to clit.

Ty's fingers in her cunt. Rob's tongue lapping her clit. Could a woman die from pleasure? If so, she was a goner. Unable to focus on anything but the sensations rushing through her body, she closed her eyes, and let her head fall back against the couch.

She was close, so close, but Rob's touch was too gentle to make her climax. Every time she felt herself about to come, the pressure eased off just enough to hold her at the edge without sending her over. She tried to lift her hips, to increase the pressure, but Rob held her down. She peeked at him through one eye, and he winked. Damn him, he was doing it on purpose.

She struggled to sit up, and both men stopped. Ty's fingers slid out of her, and Rob sat back on his heels. Rob's mouth was shiny with her juices. So was Ty's hand. They were both so hot, and delicious enough to eat, but something was wrong. "You two are wearing far too many clothes."

A huge grin crossed Rob's face, and he pulled his shirt over his head. Although she'd seen those abs a hundred times, including a few hours ago, this was different. Knowing that he was taking his clothes off for her made it so much more exciting. He hooked his thumbs in his waistband, and paused. His eyes sought hers. *Was he having second thoughts? Waiting for some signal from her?*

"Okay, Ash?"

She smiled. This was so far beyond okay she didn't have the words to describe it. Her grin must have been sufficient because he returned it with a wicked one of his own, and tugged his pants and boxers down his hips and kicked them aside. What greeted her shouldn't have been a surprise but her mouth went dry. Rob's cock was thick and strong. A drop of pre-cum appeared at the tip. *Mmm, what would that taste like?* She licked her lips and Rob groaned.

She turned towards Ty. He was wearing a button-down shirt, so the reveal was slower than Rob's had been. More deliberate. Funny how the way they undressed reflected each man's personality. After discarding his shirt, Ty gave her a slow smile, and undid the button of his jeans, then pulled them down. He tossed them aside, leaving his boxers on, of course. She should have guessed from his poker playing that he wasn't the type to show all his cards at once. She smiled, content to watch the slow strip tease. From the corner of her eye, she noticed that Rob was enjoying it too.

Ty hooked his thumbs in his boxers, then stopped. He raised a brow. She smiled in encouragement, but of course that wasn't enough for Ty. Was he waiting for her to ask? To beg? She would if necessary. She was so desperate to see both these men naked, she would do whatever it took.

"The rest?" he asked.

"All of it." Her voice was rough with desire.

"As you wish."

She liked the sound of that. It was right up there with "your wish is my command."

Where Rob's cock was thick and strong like his hands, Ty's matched his elegant fingers: long and straight as an arrow. It looked as delicious as Rob's. Would the two men taste different? Feel different? She couldn't wait to find out.

They were all naked now, but she didn't have a chance to wonder what came next. She leaned into the corner of the couch, resting against the arm while Ty knelt in front of her. His lips came down to suck on her clit. Rob walked around to her corner of the couch, and knelt on the floor. His face was level with hers. He took her mouth in a long hard kiss as Ty buried his face between her thighs. When Rob sucked softly on her tongue, Ty did the same to her clit.

Rob's hands found one of her breasts. She raised her hand to the other one, and together they pinched and rolled her nipples until pleasure radiated in waves across her chest. Ty continued his sensuous attack on her slit. When she was sure that she couldn't take another second, he grasped her hips, and pulled her forward until she was perched on the edge of the cushion. He pulled a condom from his jeans pocket. He started to tear at the corner but she put a hand over his. "I'm on the pill, and clean. You?"

Ty nodded and tossed the condom aside. With his gaze on hers, he knelt between her thighs once again, this time with his cock grasped in his hand. He'd been standing like that when she'd interrupted him in the guest room at Val's house. They were going to fuck again, but this time it wouldn't be rushed. This time she was going in with her eyes wide open – and another man at her side.

She glanced at Rob. His gaze was also fixed on Ty's cock. *Does he want to touch Ty as much as I do? To fuck and suck that gorgeous cock?* The scene from her fantasy flashed through her mind: these two men with bodies intertwined, cocks dueling between their bodies. She knew Rob would be into it.

What would Ty think? Did he know that Rob liked men? Had he noticed Rob's attention and desire? She glanced up at him. Ty was looking down at her, his gaze focused on her slit. He positioned himself at her opening, then looked at Rob

What was that about? She didn't have a chance to wonder because Ty started to enter her slowly. His cock stretched her wide, and he filled her inch-by-inch. When he was fully seated, he paused, and gave Ashley a long slow kiss. Then he leaned back, braced his hands on the cushions to either side of her hips, and started to pump into her with a strong, steady rhythm.

While Ty moved between her thighs, Rob leaned in to kiss her. He fondled her breasts with one rough hand. She could see his other hand moving too. She looked over the edge of the couch and saw that he was stroking his own cock in time with Ty's thrusts.

Holy shit, that's hot.

She watched him, her body getting hotter with each stroke of Rob's hand and Ty's cock. "Rob," she said with a gasp. She gestured at him, waving her hand up. His expression was puzzled, but he obeyed, coming to his feet. She didn't have the breath or clarity of mind to explain so she grabbed his hip, and pulled it towards her. His eyes went wide with surprise, and he pressed his hips forward, bringing his cock in range of her mouth.

She grasped Rob's cock with one hand, and paused to take a breath. He tapped her lightly on the shoulder, and she looked up. "I'm healthy too, Ash," he said, looking suddenly shy. "Just so you know."

She nodded, and turned her attention to the wonder in her hand. She licked the end, then sucked the smooth purple head between her lips. Rob slid his hands into her hair, and his eyes screwed up tight, but didn't pull her forward. She appreciated his patience. She had fantasized about Rob so many times that she wanted to take it slow. To explore the wonderful instrument of pleasure that was now in her grasp.

She licked him up one side and down the other, circled the tip with her tongue, sucked on the end until he groaned. All the while Ty's cock pumped into her, bringing her own pleasure higher and higher. Out of the corner of her eyes she saw that Ty's gaze was fixed on her, watching her suck Rob.

Ty leaned down to whisper in her ear. "You are so fucking hot, Ashley Ford." He punctuated his words with thrust, grinding his pelvis against her clit.

She gasped around the cock in her mouth, and leaned forward to take Rob completely. But he was too far away. She pulled at his hip.

"Rob," Ty said in a hoarse whisper. "She wants more."

Rob exhaled sharply, then smiled. "You can have it all, baby." He flexed his hips forward, filling her mouth completely with his warm cock. Soon his rhythm matched Ty's, one cock filling her cunt, the other in her mouth. She angled her hips up to take Ty deeper, and fisted her hand around the base of Rob's cock.

Rob stiffened, and tried to pull back, but she wouldn't let go. "Ash, I'm going to come."

Yes! she thought, but she wasn't willing to pull back long enough to speak the words. She tightened her grip, and sucked harder.

Rob tried to pull back again, but she resisted. He lost it. He thrust forward, and cried out her name. Hot cum burst into her mouth, spilling down her throat. She swallowed. Ty picked up his pace, his cock ramming into her with even greater furor. His balls slapped against her ass.

Another swallow, another thrust, and she was gone. She cried out around Rob's cock, and he stepped back, allowing it to slip from her mouth. Her hips rocketed off the couch as she flew over the edge into nirvana. Ecstasy washed over her like never before.

Tremors shook her from head to toe, radiating from her core to the ends of her limbs and back again. Her inner muscles milked Ty's cock, and he met her release with his own.

Slowly, slowly, she came back to Earth. She lay back against the cushions, unable to move a muscle. Ty sank down beside her. Rob perched on the arm of the couch. This was the awkward part. The moment when she should wonder what the hell she'd done and what would happen next. But she was tired, and far too happy to care. All she wanted now was sleep.

"Let's go to bed."

Did Rob say that or Ty? It didn't matter. She agreed completely.

Four hands tugged her gently from the couch, two strong sets of shoulders leaned against hers as they made their way to her bedroom. They had to angle sideways to fit though the door, but managed to stay connected all the way to the bed.

Rob pulled down the covers, and coaxed her gently onto the sheets. She crawled up the bed, and collapsed in the middle. Ty slipped under the covers from one side; Rob from the other. She turned on her right side, so Rob was in front of her. An arm snaked around her waist from behind and Ty pulled her close.

Rob's arm curled around her head on the pillow, his fingers resting gently against her hair. She smiled and he planted a kiss on her forehead. With her back against Ty's chest and her head resting next to Rob's, she breathed a deep sigh of contentment, and let herself drift off.

The sky was still dark when Ashley woke. A warm male body shifted behind her, a second one curled in front. The only illumination in the room came from the green glow of a digital clock, but its light didn't reach the bed.

She wasn't the only one awake. Hands roamed over her skin. One cupped her breast, another skimmed over her belly. She closed her eyes to give herself over to the sensations. A hand slipped between her thighs, brushing her clit. Fingers delved into her wet slit. A mouth nibbled on her ear.

Had Ty been sleeping behind her or Rob? Was that Rob's mouth on her shoulder, or Ty's? It was impossible to tell. It didn't matter. Lips teased her nipples, while strong hands pulled her leg up. A cock teased her slit from behind. She arched back, and it slid forward to fill her to the hilt in one smooth thrust.

One man kissed her nipples, while the other fucked her from behind. Hands massaged her breasts, held onto her hips. She reached for the cock in front of her, wrapping both hands around its hard length.

Hands. Mouths. Cocks. Her body was a stage for lust. A vessel of pure sensation.

The cock in her hand stiffened, then pulsed. Hot cum

spurted into her palms. Bodies shifted, and she wiped her hands on a corner of the sheet. She rolled onto her stomach, and the man behind her followed, his stiff cock still inside her channel. Hands gripped her hips, and she was pulled back, so that her ass stuck up in the air. The man behind her pumped harder and harder, balls slapping against her with every thrust. A hand slipped between her legs. Warm fingers stroked her lips, and found her clit. With each thrust the cock within her hit a sweet spot, forcing her clit against that hand until she came. Waves of pleasure washed over her. A few more thrusts, and she felt the cock in her pussy pulse.

Sated once again, she rolled onto her side. Again an arm banded her waist, and a forehead touched hers on the pillow. Not a single word had been spoken, but her limbs hummed with pleasure. Eyes still closed, she smiled, and fell back asleep.

Chapter Thirteen

Rob woke and stretched. He couldn't remember feeling this good in a long time. And not just physically. Something had clicked into place last night and it felt awesome. No mystery of what it was: he and Ashley had finally gotten naked together!

They hadn't been alone, but that was fine. *Damned fine.* In a million years Rob wouldn't have thought of proposing a threesome, but having Ty with them had been like the realization of a dream. Now he understood why Ashley had sex with her ex when she went back to Oak Valley, even after all that had happened between them. The man was damned near irresistible.

Rob lay back against the pillows, his morning erection tenting the sheets. Too bad the bed was empty. He was up for an encore – *another* encore – of last night's performance. Maybe Ashley and Ty could be enticed back to bed. Or they could use the couch again.

Where were they? The clock read eight-thirty. Was Ty an earlier riser? Ash certainly wasn't. A bead of worry formed in his gut, but he pushed it aside. If the smell of coffee was an indication, the others had gotten up for breakfast. He smiled. He could use a little sustenance before the next round.

Rob untangled himself from the sheets, and slipped into his bedroom to get a pair of sweatpants. Then he followed the smell of coffee to find Ashley on the couch, hands wrapped around a steaming mug.

Rob yawned. "Any more of that?"

Ashley nodded towards the kitchen, but didn't look up. *Uh oh*. He studied her from the corner of his eye. Her legs were tucked under her, and her whole body was curled inward. Not good.

He shuffled towards the coffee pot, fixed himself a cup, and took a deep draught. Only then did he turn to face whatever fallout there might be from last night's activities. "Ty gone?"

She nodded eyes on her coffee. "Took off around seven. Something about business downtown."

"In Nashville?" Ashley gave a half shrug. "Well, I hope he can function on a few hours of sleep. We didn't get too much last night."

"No, we didn't." She still didn't meet his eyes.

The knot in his stomach tightened. Time to deal with this head on. Rob put his coffee on the table, and crouched down in front of her. He placed his hands on her knees and waited until she peeked up at him. Her sleepy eyes and tumbled hair made him want to kiss her right back into bed but he resisted. "We okay, Ash?"

At first she said nothing, and Rob's heart jumped into his throat. Had he screwed everything up? He'd wanted to get physical with her, but not at the expense of what they already had.

She tilted her head, as if thinking, and gave a small smile. "Yeah, we're good. It's just..." She shrugged. "It feels kinda weird, you know? I mean I never..." her voice trailed off, and she went back to studying the mug in her hands.

Was she regretting being with him, having a threesome, or both? Rob was dying to know but didn't feel like now was the time to ask. He took a shortcut instead. "Did you enjoy it?"

She nodded. No hesitation there, thank God. "Oh yes," she added, and her breathy voice made his cock twitch. Relief flooded through Rob, followed by a pulse of desire but he pushed the latter down. "Then that's all that matters." He stood, and retrieved his coffee. "Think you'll want another cup?" It was just a formality. Ashley could never function on only one coffee.

"Of course." Her smile was bigger this time, and Rob's gut unclenched. He returned to the coffee machine to refill his mug and Ashley's, and breathed a slow sigh. There wouldn't be any encores but things were okay between him and Ashley, and that was all that mattered. *Right?*

Rob turned toward the coffee machine, and Ashley looked up. She hadn't wanted him to see the look on her face, which had to be some combination of desire, confusion and self-pity. *Why did he have to look so good first thing in the morning?* Even the mundane act of getting coffee made his muscles dance beneath his T-shirt. He wasn't wearing a shirt, and when he stretched his arms over his head, she fought the urge to run her tongue along the indent of his spine, from those strong hard shoulders to the curve of his tight muscled ass.

He turned, and she quickly looked away. With a nod he handed her the coffee cup, and headed into the bathroom. A moment later she heard the shower go on, and let out the breath she'd been holding.

So that was it - they were *okay*. She'd taken on two men at once, fucked, and sucked her ex and her best friend *at the same time*, but they'd enjoyed themselves so everything was "okay".

Really? She buried her head in her hands. She had given Rob a *blowjob*. The man she lived, and worked with everyday. He may even have fucked her – she had no idea of which one of them had been behind her in the middle of the night. What did that say about her?

And what was she going to say the next time he went out to pick up men? Did she have the right to say anything? Rob only did casual. Had last night been just another hook-up? What else could it have been, with another man there?

Not that she wanted it to be more. She and Rob were friends. Partners. Anything else would only complicate things.

And what about Ty? He'd slipped out of bed as the sun was rising, saying he had business to take care of in Nashville. Maybe he'd wanted to avoid the awkward morning-after. Well, that was fine by her. Last night didn't change the way she and Ty had left things three years ago, and she had no desire to dredge all that up again. Best to forget the whole thing.

She snorted. *As if.* Okay, if she couldn't forget it, then at least she'd vow not to do screw him a *third* time. How crazy was that? After three years of silence, she'd had sex with her ex not once, but *twice* in two days. First, like a freaking animal at Val's, then again last night. While she sucked Rob's cock. And maybe a third time in the middle of the night. *That was definitely not normal.*

She gave another snort. She'd left normal behind the moment those two men had met on her Granny's porch. She flopped back onto the couch, and looked at the ceiling. She'd wanted both Ty and Rob - *so badly* - and they'd wanted her.

There were no words to describe the pleasure they'd given her. But these morning-after regrets sucked. Why couldn't she deal with it like a guy? *Was it good for you, babe? Me too. Okay, we're cool.* She repeated those lines in her head like a mantra, but they only made her feel worse.

That was why she'd kept her distance from any romantic attachments these past few years - they fucked everything up. Distracted her from what really mattered. She should be thinking about last night's *onstage* performance, not what she'd done with Rob and Ty afterward. Focusing on music, not men. She was becoming as bad as her mother, except instead of worrying about one man, she was obsessing about two.

The shower stopped, and a few minutes later Rob came into the living room with a towel draped around his hips. She'd seen him naked before, but now she knew *exactly* what he looked like under that cloth. Had seen his large, beautiful cock up close. She closed her eyes, and bit back a groan. How was she supposed to go back to just friends now that she knew what he *tasted* liked? Just thinking about it made her hot. And sad.

When she opened her eyes, Rob was scrubbing his hair with another towel. The movement made his chest muscles ripple. She wanted to run her hands all over him, and nibble at those bronze nipples. The towel around his hips shifted precariously. It would be so easy to tug it off...

Rob cleared his throat. "Hey, Ash? Can we talk band stuff for a minute?"

Band stuff. Here she was fantasizing about getting Rob naked, and he wanted to talk business. They were going back to being Sweet Talk. Which was exactly what she wanted.

She shook her head to clear it. "What do you want to talk about?"

"I've been thinking about our next move. With the amazing show we put on last night—"

Ashley frowned. "One show doesn't mean much. Not after months of sucky performances."

"In your voicemail you told me you played well at Charley's too. That's two great performances."

"I know but the critics won't see it that way. It will take more than that to convince them–"

Rob interrupted her with a hand on her shoulder. Her womb tightened, and a shiver ran through her. He was standing exactly where he'd been last night when she'd sucked him. All she had to do is tug him closer and pull off that towel– *Focus, Ashley. This is your musical future you're talking about.* With a swallow, she forced her gaze up to his face.

Rob didn't seem to have noticed her distraction. "It's coming back, Ash. I can feel it, you can feel it, and the audience sure as hell felt it last night. You keep heading in that direction and the critics will catch up soon enough."

She shrugged, and Rob gave her a mock stern look. She nodded reluctantly.

"That's better," he said, ruffling her hair. Like a kid's. "So, as I was saying, with the amazing show we put on last night..." He paused, as if daring her to contradict his words. She didn't, and he continued. "We need to think about what we want to do next. Who we want to work with. I know we spoke about renewing Brad's contract when it runs out in two weeks, but maybe we should consider what direction we want to head in musically and professionally, and find someone who shares that vision."

"You don't think Brad shares our vision? He seems to be working pretty hard. He got us last night's gig. He's looking into that new club, too, and he's been real supportive of me, during this, um, slump..."

Ashley trailed off at the odd look that flashed across Rob's face. He looked away before she could be sure of what she saw. *Anger? Guilt?* What would Rob have to feel guilty about? "Is there something wrong, Rob?"

He shook his head, and turned back to her, his expression clear. "No. It's nothing. I'm just thinking about the future. There are so many options for musicians today outside of the traditional record labels—"

She held up a hand. "Wait a second. If you're talking about going indie, you know how I feel about that."

Rob threw up his hands. "Ashley, it's the twenty-first century. Lots of bands go indie, and do great. They get to follow their own vision, without having to be dependent on fickle record labels or two-faced agents or—"

"Two-faced agents? I knew you had doubts about working with Brad but, *two-faced?*"

Rob opened his mouth, then closed it again. He paused, as if considering his words carefully before he spoke. "Well, maybe not Brad specifically. I just meant that when you go the traditional route, there are so many middlemen. They don't care about your music or your future, only the buck they can make off you today. "

Rob had been pushing her to consider going indie for sometime now but this outburst seemed way more intense than usual. "Rob, is there something you're not telling me?"

He ran a restless hand through his wet hair, flinging drops of water everywhere. "I ran into Brad the other night at the launch party for the Hillbillies and, well, I didn't like his attitude. I don't think he's working as hard for us as you think."

Did she imagine the pause before the word *us*? "You mean

he's putting other acts before Sweet Talk?"

Again, an odd look flickered across Rob's face. He rubbed his eyes with one hand. "That's not it exactly. I just don't want to work with him anymore. I don't think he believes in us the way he used to."

He looked frustrated. She held up her hands in a reassuring gesture. "Okay. I mean if you feel that strongly about it, of course we should look for someone else."

Rob peeked out from under his hand. "Someone who works with indie artists?" She opened her mouth to protest, and he added, "Just think about it."

She sighed then nodded. Rob could be very persuasive. "Okay, I'll think about it."

"Maybe talk to some indie artists to find out about their experience?"

She pointed a finger at him. "Now you're pushing your luck."

He smiled and gave her a wink. "Always, babe." He leaned down, and kissed her on the top of her head. Ashley inhaled the scent of spicy soap mingled with the Rob's own masculine smell. Her belly tightened.

He spoke into her hair. "Ash, you're the best. You know that right?"

A tingle danced across her skin. All she had to do was tilt her face up to his. Rob pulled back, and she swallowed her disappointment. Without a backwards glance, he headed back to the bathroom. When he stepped inside, he pulled the towel off his hips. Ashley caught a glimpse of a muscled thigh and ass before the door closed.

She shook her head. *Not for you, Ashley.* Time to focus on what was solid between her and Rob: Sweet Talk and the music they made together.

Chapter Fourteen

Ty sat in the middle of a long conference table, finishing his second cup of coffee. A dozen people sat with him, looking at the PowerPoint presentation on the screen. It showed the line-up and projected attendance for the first six months of shows at the Roadhouse, a new club opening in Nashville in a few weeks.

Shortly after Ashley left Oak Valley, a friend had contacted Ty about an investment opportunity in Nashville. The closure of a recording label had freed up some space right on Music Row, and plans were being made for a new music venue. Ty had jumped at the opportunity. The fact that it would be in Nashville, the real home of Ashley's heart, was part of the attraction, of course.

A young woman came around with the coffee pot. He could use some more. He caught her eye, and gestured at his cup. He waved away her offer of milk, and took a long sip, then sat forward to recapture the thread of the discussion. The speaker leaned a hip against the table. "As you've probably all heard by now, our headliner has to undergo vocal cord surgery, and has cancelled all appearances for the next four months. That leaves us with a hole in our opening night line-up. I have a few ideas for replacements but it will be difficult to get someone else that big with so little notice."

A big man with a cowboy hat sat up. Ty recognized him as one of the other financial backers of the club. "How about The Boondocks? They're not as big but should still draw a good crowd. I don't think they're on tour right now."

A few heads nodded at the suggestion. A small intense man with red hair and a flushed face leaned forward. He was practically vibrating in his chair. "I've been thinking about another approach. We could get someone like that – or we could use this as an opportunity to do something different. Why not open that time slot to a few up-and-coming acts? They would be cheaper than one big name, and give a real music festival feel to the opening night."

More people nodded this time, including the man who had suggested The Boondocks. It was an interesting idea, but Ty would leave the final decision to the music experts. He sipped his coffee as the talk shifted to favorite local bands. A friendly debate started on the merits of Kaycee's Country Dogs versus the Townies, and Ty found his mind wandering.

A few moments later, he realized that he'd lost the thread of the conversation again. He shook his head. For the first time in his life, he was having trouble focusing on a business meeting, and it wasn't only because he was going on four hours of sleep. He couldn't stop thinking about last night.

The meeting ended, but the group was heading over to the club to check on progress there. Then he and a few other backers were meeting with the bank. With the opening coming up so quickly, there were a lot of last-minute details to be ironed out, so he'd probably be in meetings all day.

Ty grabbed a copy of the presentation and headed downstairs to his bike. He threw a leg over the seat, and immediately thought of Ashley. A memory sprang to his mind of her naked with her legs spread wide. Her pussy wrapped around him, her lips around Rob's cock. He shifted to cover the sudden tightening of his groin. Damn, it had been hot to see her take on two men like that. In the privacy of his own mind he could admit how much it had turned him on. He'd focused on Ashley's pleasure, but he couldn't deny that the other man had drawn his attention too. Rob definitely reminded Ty of Matt, and it wasn't just his looks. Ty felt the same strange attraction for Rob, but he wasn't a confused teenager anymore. This time around he knew exactly what he was feeling. *Lust.*

He sat back on the bike. *What would Rob say if he knew?* Now that Ty had spent a little time with him, he didn't think Rob was narrow-minded, but that was a far cry from being interested in guys. Not that he was interested in Rob. Ty knew that he was straight, not gay or bi. If he'd enjoyed watching Rob with Ashley, that was part of what had made the evening so amazing. An experience he definitely wanted to repeat.

He wished that he hadn't had to take off so early. He'd have loved to wake up in bed with Ashley, and take her again in the daylight, with eyes wide open. He chuckled softly to himself. Not that they hadn't enjoyed themselves the second time in the dark.

He pulled out his mobile phone. He'd sent her a *good morning* text but she hadn't replied. He dialed her number but his call went to voicemail.

They must be awake by now. A seed of worry grew in his mind. His early disappearance this morning could easily be misconstrued. Especially by a woman as skittish as Ashley. Would she think that he was having regrets? Was she? That was his real fear – that in the cold light of day Ashley would regret what had happened between the three of them. Worse, she would use it as an excuse to run away. Again.

He had no intention of letting *that* happen.

Of course, they needed to talk. To clear the air about what happened between them three years ago. He remembered that painful night too clearly. Ashley had come to him excited about Rob's offer, but all he could hear was that she was going. Leaving to follow dreams that suddenly didn't include him. When he hadn't shared her enthusiasm, she'd accused him of not believing in her. That couldn't have been further from the truth, and he should have told her that, right then and there. But all he could see was that the woman he had made love to all year long was being lured away by a sweet-talking pretty boy with a one-way ticket to Nashville.

Instead he'd argued with her. Tried to talk her out of it. Told her that he was concerned about Rob's intentions – which he had been – but it all came out wrong. By morning, he realized that he might have sounded too harsh, but it was too late. She'd taken off without another word, and refused his calls. Ignored his texts.

By some miracle, she was back. Back in his life. Back in his bed. He didn't know where this was going, or what would happen next, but one thing he knew for sure – he was not going to let Ashley Ford leave him behind again.

Chapter Fifteen

Rob couldn't deny it any longer – the afternoon practice wasn't going well. They'd been going for three hours now, and Ashley had seemed distracted the whole time, stumbling over lyrics, and missing cues. Was it a delayed reaction to what they'd done together last night, or something else?

Rob glanced over to where Brad sat at the bar. His face was a pleasant mask, but Rob knew that looks were deceiving with that guy. He hated that their manager was hearing this practice – it would only reinforce the concerns he had voiced about Ashley last week.

They played "Cherry Pie" again. It was one of Ashley's favorite songs, one that had blown the audience away Sunday night. It sounded pretty good the second time, but nothing like the fiery performance she'd given at Bootleggers. Nothing like the passion she'd shown onstage and with him and Ty later that night. Was she regretting what had happened between them? They hadn't spoken of it beyond their conversation this morning. In fact, she hadn't said much to him since then.

They played a few more songs. The whole band seemed to have caught Ashley's mood, and every song sounded flat, until they got to the last one. "No One to Call Me Mine" was a semi-solo that featured Ashley on guitar with a little percussion. It sounded great. Soulful, passionate, and terribly, terribly sad. No one else seemed to appreciate the irony that her playing only came alive for an unhappy song. The band looked relieved, and even Brad seemed to relax a bit. But Ashley's mood ate away at Rob like a cancer.

He put his guitar aside, and made his way towards her. She hadn't moved since the song ended, just sat there worrying her lower lip with her teeth. Although he knew that she did that when she was nervous or upset, he'd always found the action arousing, which only proved what an insensitive oaf he was. He shook his head. It was a miracle he hadn't screwed things up before this.

He stepped over an amp, and his foot hit an empty coffee cup. It skittered across the floor, landing at Ashley's feet. She looked up, bringing her lips together in a firm line. Rob ignored the sick feeling in his gut, and forced himself to smile. "Sounded great on that last song, Ash."

She gave a bitter laugh. "Thanks."

They stood in awkward silence for a moment. Rob cleared his throat. "Let's get out of here. We can stop by the grocery store, whip up some dinner, then head over to the Divas' show at Gracie's."

Ashley frowned. "I forgot the Divas' show was tonight. I'm not really up for going out – I may be coming down with something."

Rob knew what she was coming down with – a bad case of the regrets. He'd love to suggest the hair of the dog as a cure, but that would probably make things worse. Instead, he forced himself to smile. "Come on, Ash. It will be fun. Besides, you know how much it means to them to have us there."

The male lead of the band wasn't officially out, but the rumors had been enough to get the Divas dumped from their label for not being "family-friendly." Since then Rob and Ashley had made a point of attending shows whenever they could, and had become good friends with the band members.

A guilty look crossed Ashley's face, but she shook her head. "Not tonight, Rob. Could you give them my apologies?"

Rob gave a reluctant nod. If guilt couldn't get her to come out with him, nothing would short of tying her up and tossing her over his shoulder. He doubted that would improve things.

She got up, and shook out her hair. "I'm going to wash up, and run some errands on the way home. I'll see you later, okay?"

With that dismissal, she headed for the bathroom. Rob fought the urge to follow her – he was probably the last person she wanted to be with right now. He mentally kicked himself for putting them in this position. They'd lived together for three years, and he'd managed to keep his feelings and the attraction he felt for her under control. He'd known that acting on them could backfire. What had changed? Why had he let things go so far this time?

Ty. As always it came back to him. When Rob had heard that she'd slept with her ex, and saw her kiss Ty before the show, something in Rob had snapped. He'd let jealousy and possessiveness overcome years of caution – and this was the result. He kicked himself again.

Rob returned to his guitar, packed it away, and stormed toward the door. Brad fell into step beside him. *Damn.* Rob was not in the mood to deal with the manager's crap right now.

They stepped out of the bar, and into the late afternoon sun. Before Rob could escape, Brad spoke. "So what did you think of the practice?"

Rob gritted his teeth. Even though Ashley had been amazing Sunday night, Rob knew the manager would see today's practice as proof that she was still in a slump. "She sounded great on that last song." His tone dared Brad to disagree.

Brad nodded. "Of course she did – she sounded the way she used to. The way she should have for every other song you practiced. After Sunday's show I was hoping we'd put the problems behind us, but it doesn't seem that way." Brad rubbed a hand over his face. Rob had never seen the manager lose his cool even that much. The guy was really worried.

Brad looked at him again. "She was distracted the whole time, screwing up on songs that she wrote. This isn't good, Rob. I'm trying to get recording studios interested in you guys, but I can't invite them to shows if she's going to play like that. They're expecting to see star material. Someone worthy of major time and investment."

Rob jabbed a finger at Brad. "She was amazing Sunday night. You said so yourself."

"She was fantastic, but one night isn't enough. She needs to be that good *every* time. The studios want consistency. A star who can wow them night after night, album after album. Not once in a while, or when the mood strikes." Brad looked up for a moment, as if thinking, then nodded at Rob. "I have an idea. Ashley needs a little space now. Maybe we can take the pressure off her a bit by focusing the attention on you. Letting the execs get to know the Rob Porter half of Sweet Talk a bit better." He nodded again. "Yes, that could work."

What did that mean? "Get to know me better? Why? Ashley and I are equal members of Sweet Talk."

Brad raised a placating hand. "I know. I know. It would be a temporary thing, just to give the execs something to think about while Ashley deals with whatever is bothering her."

Rob could almost see the gears turning in Brad's mind. He was still skeptical, but if Brad's plan would buy time for Ashley, it was worth a try. Brad raised his brows in question, and Rob nodded. He felt a niggling sense of doubt at the relieved look on Brad's face.

What had he just agreed to?

Later that night Rob climbed the stairs to the apartment, stifling a yawn. As promised, he'd gone to the Divas' show, but left early. The band members had been surprised. The open secret that the lead singer was gay drew lots of hot available men into the ranks of their fans, and Rob had often hooked up at their shows. But tonight he hadn't been in the mood.

Kyle had been there too. After Ashley's cold shoulder, Rob had been briefly tempted to go home with his former lover, even if only to wipe the memory of what he *couldn't* have from his mind. But when all he could think of were red hair, and a hard cock pumping in and out of Ashley's slit, he'd turned Kyle down.

Rob dug the keys out of his pocket, and unlocked the front door. The living room was dark. He headed towards the bathroom, slowing as he reached Ashley's door. He was about to walk past when a strip of light appeared beneath it.

"I'm up," a voice called from within.

He knew he shouldn't torture himself, but he couldn't resist. He opened the door, and caught his breath. Ashley was struggling to sit up, her rumpled hair and rough voice suggesting that she had been asleep moment ago. Both reminded him too clearly of what they'd been doing last night. What he wanted to do again right now. His cock pulsed behind his fly.

She pushed herself higher on the pillows. "How was the show?"

He shrugged. "Good. You should have come."

Her mouth quirked in a half-smile. "It was more your scene than mine."

Rob didn't know what that meant so he let it slide. "So how are you feeling?"

"Huh? Oh, better. Thanks."

An awkward silence stretched between them. He rubbed a hand over his eyes. Is this how things would be from now on? He hoped not.

Ashley cleared her throat. "So, meet anyone interesting?"

"Huh?"

"You know." She gave an odd laugh. "Was he blond or a brunette this time?"

Rob froze, and slowly brought his hand away from his face. He stared but her eyes only widened, a look of mock lechery on her face.

She had to be kidding. "You think I picked someone up tonight? Got laid?"

Ashley shrugged, looking uncomfortable. "It was a Divas' party after all..." Her voice trailed off.

He spoke without thinking. "But that was before."

She looked up, brow knotted in confusion. "Before?"

His heart dropped into his stomach, and disappointment crashed over him. Even though Ashley had retreated this morning, and seemed to regret what they'd done, he'd unconsciously started thinking of their relationship in terms of *before* and *after*. He opened his mouth to speak, but what could he say? *You know, before we had sex. Before everything changed between us.* She obviously didn't see it the same way. Better yet: *Didn't that mean anything to you?* No way was he going to say that. He'd sound like a chick.

With nothing to say, he turned, and stalked out of her room. He charged into the bathroom, closing the door behind him, barely holding himself back from slamming it. Bracing his hands on the sink, he stared into the mirror.

In spite of her morning-after reaction, on some deep level Rob had kept his fingers crossed that the other night had been a turning point for them. That once she'd gotten over her shock they could explore this new dimension in their relationship. But that desire only went one way. If he'd needed a clear sign that the other night meant nothing to her, well, he'd gotten it. What had he expected? They'd lived together for three years. If she were going to express an interest, surely it would have happened by now.

Fuck! For one blessed, heart-stopping, lust-inducing moment, everything had felt perfect. He'd been naked in bed with Ashley, *and* another man. Sharing her like that... *Damn*. And Ty was seriously pretty himself, even if Rob didn't like him very much. The only thing that would have made it perfect was for Ty to be into him as well.

But it didn't matter 'cause Rob had been kidding himself. Ashley wasn't interested in him beyond a one-night stand, and who knew what the hell Ty was thinking, or if Rob would ever hear from him again. No, Rob would go back to being Ashley's singing partner and buddy, getting his kicks at the bars. That sounded exactly as exciting and fulfilling as it had always been. *Not.*

That used to be enough though, hadn't it? Sex with men, casual and plentiful. Could he go back to it, now that he'd had a taste of something more? He paused, shaking his head as a sad realization dawned on him. Casual sex had never been enough. It had just been a placeholder, a consolation prize when, after holding out for years, he'd finally accepted that he couldn't have the person he really wanted.

Holy shit, it was all becoming clear. His eyes widened in the mirror. Ashley had wondered why he never went for women, even though he said he was bi. Now he knew why. Because somehow, when he hadn't been paying attention, something had happened. Something he would never have expected. He'd fallen in love with Ashley Ford.

And now that he'd gotten a taste of her, he was supposed to go back to casual hook-ups? *Fuck no*. Not without a fight.

Rob pulled the door open with far more force than required, stepped out, and stopped. Ashley was standing in her doorway. Her head was tilted down, and she looked up at him from beneath her lashes. She wore the T-shirt he'd taken off Sunday night. The hem ended mid-thigh showing a long expanse of bare leg.

"Rob?" Her voice was tentative.

Rob took a deep breath. Seeing her wrapped in his clothes calmed his anger a bit, but stoked another kind of fire. "That's my shirt."

She looked down, and a flush spread across her face. "Yeah. I, um..."

"I like it on you."

She smiled shyly – *Ashley shy?* – and looked at her feet. "I'm sorry."

He raised a brow but said nothing.

She peeked up at him with a shrug. "That's how it always went, you know. You went out, and got some, and we talked afterwards. Now, I don't know what to do, what comes... after." She waved a hand in the air, a confused expression on her face.

Rob exhaled as his whole body sighed with relief. "Me neither, Ash. But I won't go back."

She looked up at that, her eyes wide with surprise, and something else. Before Rob could figure out what it was, she looked over her shoulder then back at her feet.

An invitation? He stepped forward, and she turned, fleeing into the room.

Rob paused for a moment, then stepped through the door. Ashley perched on the edge of her bed. She peeked up at him again, her fingers worrying the hem of the T-shirt. The shirt bunched up on her legs, and Rob could see auburn curls peeking out of the valley of her thighs. His cock stirred, but he forced himself to move slowly until he was standing in front of her. Now that she wasn't trying to escape, he could be patient.

He didn't have to wait long. She cleared her throat. "I used to think about it, you know. When you went out – and when you came home." She looked down at her feet.

Think about what?

She raised her gaze to him. There was no mistaking the lust in her eyes. His balls pulled up tight. "What did you think about." It wasn't a question – it was a demand.

Her voice came out in a whisper that sent erotic shivers across his skin. "About you and the men you... I fantasized about you with them."

Holy shit. The breath left Rob's chest in a sharp whoosh. She'd fantasized about him. With men. It took a moment for his brain to form coherent thoughts. He swallowed. "What did you imagine us doing?"

She tilted her head to the side considering the question, and Rob's knees almost buckled from the look on her face – a sexy-as-hell combination of innocent concentration and lust. "Well, I didn't know if you liked giving or receiving, so I imagined both."

Blood rushed to Rob's cock. Spots danced before his eyes. "I like both."

Her eyes widened, and her tongue darted out to lick her lips. "Does it feel good?" she asked, and laughed softly. "Of course it does or else you wouldn't do it."

"You mean you've never done it—"

"In the backdoor?" she said, making quotes with one hand. "No." She was clearly embarrassed, but if the nipples poking against his T-shirt were anything to go by, she was turned on too.

Rob reached for the curl of red hair that lay temptingly across her breast, and pulled it gently through his fingers. "It feels good Ash. Real good." She looked up at him, her pupils so dilated that her green irises were barely visible. He leaned closer. "Let me show you how good it feels."

She nodded.

Whoa. That was a lot easier than he'd expected. He took a deep breath, counting backwards from ten. As eager as she seemed, he had to take it slow. He took a step back, and pointed at the T-shirt. "Take it off."

Her nostrils flared, and her hands went to the bottom hem. Gaze locked on his face, she peeled the shirt up, revealing damp curls, a smooth stomach, and finally round, pink-tipped breasts, with peaked nipples. A surge of lust flared in his groin, and he fought the urge to toss her onto the bed, and take her right then and there. He counted from ten again, then leaned down, and pressed his mouth against hers. She opened her mouth to him, and her arms came up to wrap around his shoulders. Before he could steady himself, she flopped back onto the mattress, pulling him down with her.

Rob covered her body with his, laying claim to every glorious inch. He was done playing it safe. Letting another man take what he had wanted for so long.

Tonight, Ashley Ford was his.

Chapter Sixteen

Ashley pulled Rob against her. She'd wanted him for too long to hold back. She needed him in her bed, in her body, right here and now. She would deal with the fallout tomorrow.

Rob gave her a passionate kiss, then rolled onto his back. He pulled off his shirt, and made quick work of his pants and boxers until he was as naked as she was. He turned back to her, his cock pressed eagerly into her hip. His hands came up to her breasts, kneading them softly, while he captured a nipple in his mouth. A flick of his tongue sent sparks through her body. He switched to the other breast, and did the same. His actions felt wonderful but she wasn't in the mood for foreplay. Rob had promised her something far more exciting, and she was eager to get to it.

She fisted a hand in his hair, and tugged until his lips came off her nipple with a soft, wet pop. With a laugh, he lay back. His hand skimmed down her body, and over her belly. He continued south, and her body tingled with anticipation. She spread her legs to allow him greater access. His hand moved over her damp curls, and down to her lower lips, and clit. He flicked her gently, and pleasure shot through her.

With his gaze on her pussy, Rob kneeled between her thighs.

His lips came down on her, and his tongue stroked her clit. The bolt of pleasure shot through, so strong it made her whole body shudder. He continued to lap and lick, and soon she was squirming against the sheets.

Rob slipped a finger inside her, and made a low growl. She could feel the sound vibrate against her damp flesh. "Damn, Ash, you are so wet. I want to fuck you here too, but we have other plans tonight." He pulled his hand back, and looked up at her. "Do you have any lube?"

"In there." She pointed to the table at the side of the bed.

He pulled open the drawer, and a curious look came over his face. Before Ashley could figure out what had him so intrigued, he reached in, and pulled out a large pink satin pouch. He untied the drawstring, and took out the long purple vibrator she'd used the other night. He flicked the switch. It buzzed to life, and her cheeks flamed.

He held up the toy. "Did you use this when you fantasized? About me with other men?"

She squirmed and nodded. "Sometimes."

He groaned, closing his eyes before turning the toy off, and returning it to the satin bag. "I want to see that sometime. You pleasuring yourself."

The implication that there would be more times after this made her dizzy for a moment. "Really?"

"Babe, that would be so fucking hot. But not tonight. We've got a date for something else." He put the vibrator back in the drawer, and pulled out a small bottle of lube.

Show time. She was excited, but nervous too. Before she could reconsider, she turned onto her stomach, and got up on her hands and knees.

Rob chuckled, and rubbed her ass with one hand. "Damn,

Ash, I could look at your beautiful, *fuckable* ass all day. But we'll do it the other way this time, so I can see your face."

There was another way? She looked over her shoulder at him, confused. "The other way?"

He shook his head. "Wow, you really are an innocent. An anal virgin." She nodded. He kissed her left ass cheek, then gave it a gentle swat. "Lay on your back, babe and spread your legs wide for me."

She did as he instructed. He crawled between her thighs. "Now pull your knees up and grab your shins."

Oh. This position pulled her pussy and her ass cheeks apart, exposing her completely while allowing her to see Rob's face.

He looked down at her, staring at her pussy and ass so long she'd have worried that he was reconsidering if not for the naked desire in his face. He shook his head. "Ash, you have no idea of how long I've fantasized about this."

Her mind couldn't even begin to grasp the implications of that statement. "Really?"

He gave a laugh. "Oh yeah." He squirted lube on his fingers, and rubbed the clear gel between his fingers. One hand came down to stroke her clit again, while the other reached for her sensitive back hole. With two fingers he circled her pucker with warm, slippery lube. The novel contact sent tingles through her body, and her inner muscles quivered.

He squirted more lube onto his hand, and pressed lightly on her anus with one finger until the tip slid in. It didn't hurt, but her muscles tightened around him automatically. He stopped.

"Relax. It feels good, doesn't it?"

It did. She nodded, took a deep breath, and her muscles released their death grip.

He pulled the tip out, then pressed in again, out and in,

out and in until she was squirming again. "How are you feeling now?" he asked, but from the smile on his face he knew.

"Amazing," she said on a gasp. "Incredible." Even better than she'd expected. No wonder Rob had sought out other men night after night. If a single finger felt this good, she couldn't wait to feel the rest of him. A second finger joined the first, and repeated the in and out motion with both, stretching her until her whole body was tingling. She let out a moan.

He pulled his fingers out, and she gave him a mock pout. He reached for his pants pocket, and pulled out a condom. She propped herself up on her elbows so she could watch him put it on. *Damn, had he always been that big?* She swallowed. *Would it even fit?* Rob must have seen the fear in her face. He paused, and laid a hand on her cheek. "We don't have to do this. It's okay if you've changed your mind."

She shook her head. "I haven't. I mean, I still want you. I'm just worried about the, er, logistics. You're so big."

He smiled. "It will fit, and it will feel good. I promise. We'll take it slow, okay?"

She nodded. He stretched the condom over his erection, and took his cock in his fist. His other hand grasped her thigh.

"It's going to be tight at first, and may sting a bit, but it gets better. A lot better." He slathered more lube on his cock, waited for her to nod again, and touched his tip to her back entrance. Her whole body quivered from that light touch

Again he paused. "If you want to stop say so, and I'll stop. Okay?"

She huffed in exasperation. "Rob, I can't tell you to stop if you don't start. *Please.*"

She felt his body shudder, and he pushed forward. Her muscles tightened again, and she took a deep breath, willing her body to relax. After a moment, she nodded to let him know it was okay to continue.

He pressed forward, stretching her wider. She felt a burning sensation, along with a tingle.

"Damn, Ashley, you are tight. Are you okay?"

She nodded. "More."

"Your wish is my command, beautiful." There was a sharp stinging sensation, and the head of his cock slipped inside. She gasped.

"Okay?"

She held up one hand, and breathed. Rob watched her patiently. After a moment, the stinging feeling subsided, replaced by a pleasurable sensation that she had never felt before. She pressed towards him, eager to feel more.

He pushed then paused. She nodded. He did it again. With each thrust her body stretched to accommodate him, and he penetrated deeper. Pleasure radiated out from her ass to her clit and slit. Her nipples tingled.

He braced his hands on her shins, and pressed forward again and again, inch by inch until his balls pressed against her skin. She felt stretched out. Full. Sparks of pleasure rippled from her ass to her clit and beyond. Even her nipples tingled. All the times she'd fantasized about Rob and his partners, she'd never imagined it could feel this good. "Wow."

He was panting, like he'd run a race. He shook his head. "Yeah, wow. I can't believe you took all of me your first time. How does it feel?"

"Good. Really good." That hardly described it but she couldn't think. Her brain and body were overwhelmed by sensation. "You?"

"Are you kidding me? I'm looking down at your beautiful

body, and my cock is buried in your tight little ass. Nothing has ever felt as good as this, Ash. *Nothing.*" His eyes blazed.

He pulled back an inch, then pressed in again. She moaned in approval. He did it again, pulling back a bit further. When they'd established a rhythm, one of his hands left her shin, and found her clit. He circled the swollen bud. "Damn Ash. If I only could fuck you, and suck you here at the same time… I bet that would feel good, eh?"

At the same time? He couldn't, but two men could. She filed the idea away for another time.

Rob had been moving slowly up until now, withdrawing only an inch or two before pushing back inside. Careful. Controlled. It felt great but Ashley was ready for more. She rocked her hips to meet his next thrust, and squeezed her muscles around him.

Rob's mouth dropped open, and his eyes closed. His hand gripped her thigh. "God, Ash."

She wasn't sure how to interpret his reaction. "Did that feel good?"

"Good?" He gave a shallow laugh. "We passed 'good' a long time ago. That felt amazing."

She smiled, and braced her hands on the bed to get better traction. She rocked to meet each thrust, pushing him deeper. Rob got the hint. He picked up his pace.

A fantastic pressure built within her. Rob called her name, locking his gaze on hers. He thrust, pinched her clit, and she was gone. Her whole body stiffened, and she cried out. It was an orgasm unlike any other she'd ever experienced. Pleasure sparked from her clit, and her ass. She felt the ecstasy in her pussy too, and her inner muscles clenched. The muscles of her ass tightened around Rob's cock, and he joined her with a cry of his own. She could feel his cock pulse against the tight skin of her behind. The vibrations set off a second wave of pleasure, which left her whole body buzzing.

Rob withdrew, and got up to discard the condom. When he returned Ashley pulled back the covers. He slipped in beside her, spooning her close.

Her body still tingled with the aftermath of her climax. Even stronger than that was the feeling that gripped her heart. She and Rob belonged together – as singing partners, *and* lovers. She didn't know where things would go from here, or what would happen tomorrow morning but one thing was sure he was in her blood now, as much a part of her as her music. And she didn't plan to give up either one.

Chapter Seventeen

Ty stopped his motorcycle in front of Ashley and Rob's apartment building. He hadn't spoken to Ashley since he'd left here yesterday morning, and she hadn't answered his call or texts. He'd tried to get away sooner to see her, but his meetings had gone late last night, and started again early this morning. So here he was, outside her apartment a day and a half after leaving her bed. He could have called ahead, but he didn't want to give her a chance to bolt. Or tell him that the other night had been a mistake. Sure, she'd been eager then, but who knew what was going through her head now. And Rob? Ty had no idea of what to think about that guy. Best not to think about him at all.

Ty climbed the exterior stairs, and located the apartment. He raised his hand but the door opened before he could knock. Rob stood in the doorway. He was shirtless, and held a basketball against his hip.

"Ty." Rob's tone was neutral, and Ty couldn't read anything in his expression.

Ty acknowledged the greeting with a lift of his chin. They stared at each other, then Rob stepped forward, pulling the door shut behind him. Ty held his ground, and for a moment the two men stood nose-to-nose. Ty could feel the other man's body heat, and the press of a muscular thigh against his, and his cock stirred to life. *What the hell?* Ty shifted his weight back to minimize the contact, but he held his ground. No way was he going to be the first to step back.

Rob broke the impasse with a sound that was somewhere between a growl and a grunt, and pressed the ball into Ty's gut. Ty grabbed it, and Rob brushed past him, pausing on the landing to toss a challenging smirk over his shoulder.

Ty returned the look. They were taking it outside.

He followed Rob down the stairs, and around the building, to a rough asphalt rectangle. A basketball hoop with a frayed net stood at one end. Rob walked to the center of the court, and turned to face Ty, planting his feet wide. Ty checked the ball to Rob, and pulled off his jacket. He dropped it at his feet, and tossed his phone and keys on top of it. Rob tossed the ball back to him, then bounced in place, shaking out his arms and loosening up.

Ty dribbled the ball, taking a moment to study his opponent from the corner of his eye. Of course he'd caught glimpses of Rob's body while they were with Ashley the other night, but in the afternoon sunlight his chest seemed more solid and muscled…

"Hey." Rob waved his hand. "Are we playing or not?"

Ty shook the distraction away, and rolled his shoulders. He dribbled the ball a few times, and started down the court. Rob laughed and followed.

Everywhere Ty went Rob was there. Ty jumped for the net. Rob was right under him. In his face. Chest to chest. Ty turned his back, and Rob's arms curved around him, his solid, sweaty pecs rubbing Ty's shoulder blades. Was he bumping and brushing Ty more than usual in a game, or was Ty just more aware of it because he'd been naked with the other man?

Sweat ran down Ty's back. He pulled off his shirt and tossed it to the side. He turned back to his opponent. But Rob wasn't looking at his face. Instead the other man's gaze traveled over Ty's body from head to toe and back. When he reached Ty's face, he smiled and turned away.

Blood pounded in Ty's ears and his cock twitched. *Had Rob just checked him out?*

Ty took a deep breath, went for the shot and missed. Now Rob had the ball. He dribbled with one hand. The other reached down to his crotch, and adjusted his junk. But instead of pulling it away, as men usually did, the hand lingered a moment, drawing Ty's attention. Was that the outline of an erection under Rob's shorts? Was this game turning him on? Before Ty could react, Rob dove to the side, and around Ty, and up to the net where he sank the ball with one hand. Rob caught the ball as it fell.

He paused, breath heaving, and grinned at Ty. "Dude, you're supposed to keep your eye on *this* ball."

And now Rob was flirting with him. Heat bloomed in Ty's chest. His gut tightened. *What was going on?* Rob's attitude went beyond the singer's previous cockiness, and there was an added swagger in his step. Was it because of what they'd done the other night – or had something else happened between Rob and Ashley while Ty was gone? The thought of them together had provoked jealousy in Ty back in Oak Valley, but now all he could think of was how hot Ashley had looked when she took Rob into her mouth.

Rob took advantage of Ty's distraction to make another basket.

Ty caught the ball before it bounced off the court. He took

a deep breath. He had to pull it together. Focus on the ballgame, not whatever mindgame Rob was playing.

He turned his back, dribbling out of Rob's reach, but Rob crowded behind him. His chest bumped Ty's back. His hips grazed Ty's ass. Blood rushed to Ty's cock, and his balls got tight. Rob bumped him again, and Ty felt the hard length of an erection prod his hip. His dick pulsed, and he swallowed, but kept control of the ball.

From the corner of his eye, Ty saw Ashley's little blue Honda pull into the lot. She got out of her car, and approached the court, a bag of groceries under each arm. Rob glanced over at her. Ty took the opportunity to slip past Rob's guard, but the other man slid between him and the net, and almost knocked the jump shot away. Damn he was fast, but Ty was faster. The score was now two to one, Rob.

Ashley watched them, a confused frown on her face. After a moment she shook her head, and headed for the stairs. Ty wondered what she was thinking but couldn't focus on her – the man in front of him demanded all of his attention. Ty faked right, then slipped around Rob to make the basket. Now they were tied. Rob leaned over, bracing his hands on his knees, his breath coming fast.

"Ashley's home," Rob said.

Ty grunted at the obvious statement. The singer looked up with a half-smile, and something shifted in Ty's chest. Rob's grin widened, and the warm feeling dropped to Ty's groin.

He glanced over to where Ashley was climbing the stairs, then back at Rob. Maybe Rob wasn't playing a game. Maybe something else was going on here. Between them. With Ashley. Ty had no idea of what it could be, but damn was he looking forward to finding out.

♫

Ashley set the grocery bag on the counter, and took a deep breath. Rob and Ty were outside, playing basketball of all things. Shirtless. Sweaty. Pushing and shoving. She could have stared at them all day except the ice cream in her grocery bag was melting. *She'd* been melting just watching them.

She was no basketball expert but from what she could see, that hadn't been just a friendly game. There had been something else in the air between them, something masculine and oh so sexy.

She heard the door open, and heavy footsteps came in. Someone came up behind her, and hands landed on her waist. The smell and heat of a man filled her senses.

"Ash." Rob's breath tickled her ear. Goosebumps rose on her arms, and her skin tingled beaded. She should have been turned off by his proximity, sweaty and dirty from playing, but she'd be damned if she wasn't finding those very things arousing.

She glanced at the doorway where Ty stood. He was naked from the waist up, wiping his brow with his balled-up shirt. Ashley's mouth went dry. When he finished he tossed the shirt on the overnight bag at his feet, and stared at her. Heat flared in his eyes, along with a question. A dare.

The hands on her waist started to turn her around, but she slipped away, and took a few steps back. She needed a moment to think. "I have to put the groceries way," she said, and pointed at the hallway. "Take a shower. Both of you."

Ty gave her a slow smile that made tiny jolts of pleasure dance along her skin. "Want to join us?"

Her belly muscles trembled. Too bad the shower couldn't

fit all of them. She shook her head, and again pointed to the hallway. "Shower."

Rob's knowing laugh carried over his shoulder. He passed Ty, and waved him to follow. "Come on. There are two bathrooms."

Ty gave her a look long hot look, and followed Rob down the hall.

Ashley tried to ignore the sounds of the shower, and the thought of the two naked wet bodies down the hall. Yes, she wanted them, but she wanted something else too, something more. She wasn't sure what that was, but after what she and Rob had experienced last night, the closeness she'd felt, she knew it went beyond another round of hot sex with Rob and Ty. Not that that would be a bad thing.

She put the food away, rescuing the ice cream before it turned to soup. Only then did she pull out the newspaper that she'd picked up at the store. Brad had sent them a text this morning about a good review in the *Music City Weekly*, and Ashley had picked up a copy of the paper while she was out.

The *Weekly* was a free paper that covered Nashville's country scene, from big names to up-and-coming acts like Sweet Talk. To land even a few lines in the paper was a big deal. Thanks to Ashley's slump, their last review of Sweet Talk had been less than stellar so she was curious to see what they'd written this time.

She found it on page sixteen, in the *Musical Notes* column. "Sweet Talk's Rob Porter was hotter than ever opening for We Were Angels last night, and Ashley Ford showed a fire that's been noticeably absent from her recent shows."

She smiled. It was a backwards compliment but she couldn't complain – it was the truth after all. She read on. "The duo practically melted the crowd with a show-stopping final kiss.

Could romance with Rob be the kindling that stoked Ashley back to life?"

Could that be it? She'd gotten that backrub from Rob before the show, and with Ty… She chuckled. Maybe Rob was right – sex was good for her creativity. If that was true then their next show should be Grammy material.

Rob emerged from the hall, toweling his hair dry. He wore a pair of jeans and a tee shirt. His feet were bare. She smiled. Rob came over to her, tossing the towel aside before wrapping his arms around her. She put her hands on his face, and kissed him hard, then leaned back to look at him. His eyes were as wide as his smile.

She pushed the paper at him. "Check this out."

His smile got wider. "I stoked you back to life, eh?" He punctuated his question with a thrust of his hips. "Sounds like fun."

"What sounds like fun?" Ty asked from the doorway.

Rob turned to him, keeping one arm around her waist. It was the same position they'd been in on Granny's porch but the mood couldn't be more different. Had that only been a few days ago?

He held the paper out to Ty. "Check out this awesome review of Sweet Talk. Page sixteen."

Ty took the paper. His brows rose as he read. He smiled. "Very nice. Congratulations."

Rob let go of her, and stepped back. She turned to Ty. "Sorry I didn't return your text. I…" She shook her head. She wasn't sure what had stopped her. She'd been so confused the morning he left, but she was really happy to see him. That had to mean something, but she wasn't sure what.

Rob spoke. "So what kept you in Nashville yesterday?"

"I'm an investor in a project downtown. Had back-to-back meetings all day."

Was this Ty's mysterious out-of-town project? The reason they'd seen a Fat Boy on Music Row? Ashley opened her mouth to ask, but Rob spoke up first. He had a gleam in his eye, and his voice dropped into that sexy range he used for love songs and ballads. "A new challenge?"

"Something like that." Ty's tone held something she couldn't name. She had no idea of what was going on between the two men but it was making the temperature climb in spite of the A/C. She pressed her thighs together, and swallowed.

Rob and Ty stared at one another for a long moment, then both men smiled. The tension dissipated, but didn't disappear, like a banked fire that could be coaxed to life in a heartbeat.

Rob nodded at Ty. "You have good timing – Ash and I were about to make dinner."

We were?

Ty grinned. "Like you showed up just in time at Granny's?"

Rob nodded, and headed for the kitchen. "We still have those steaks you picked up the other day, Ash. We could fire up the grill."

And just like that, the three of them settled into dinner prep, Ty working the grill on the balcony, and Rob seasoning the steaks while Ashley pulled together a salad and washed some sweet potatoes. Everything felt so normal that she could almost believe that she'd imagined being naked in bed with these men two days ago. Her inner muscles clenched. No, she hadn't imagined it. She couldn't possibly forget. Nor could she forget that Rob had been inside her body last night, and she'd woken up in his arms. So why was he so calm about Ty's presence?

Rob stepped back into the kitchen, and the first few bars

of Johnny Cash's "Walk the Line" sounded from his pocket. He fished out his phone, and checked the screen. "I'll be right back." He left the room.

Ty pulled three beers from the fridge while Ashley set the table, like they'd been doing it forever. It felt good to be with Ty like this. Comfortable. Not a word she would have associated with him. Their year together had been passionate, and exciting, the runaway feelings he'd inspired almost frightening in their intensity. There had been nothing "comfortable" about it. She gave Ty a sideways glance. Was she playing with fire, letting him back into her life?

As if he could hear her thoughts, Ty looked up. A soft smile played on his lips. Lips she felt a sudden urge to nibble. She looked away.

"Ashley." He moved closer, and put a hand on her arm.

She looked up. His blue gaze searched her face. "I've missed you. A lot." He swallowed. "For three years." His voice had an odd quality to it, a sense of vulnerability that she'd never heard from him before. Her throat tightened, and tears gathered in her eyes. When Ty had said that he'd followed her career all this time, she realized that her understanding of their break-up had been flawed. Hearing him say that he'd missed her confirmed it. She threw herself against his chest, and his arms tightened around her back.

Footsteps sounded across the living room, and Rob entered the kitchen with his cellphone in his hand. When he saw them, he stopped. "Am I interrupting anything?" He didn't seem surprised to see them embracing. Had he left the room to let her and Ty talk?

Ashley stepped back, wiping her eyes with the back of a hand. "Just clearing up a, er, little misunderstanding."

Ty raised a brow at the word *little*, but didn't say anything.

Rob glanced at Ty, who nodded. "Then, I'm glad you straightened it out. Anyway, that was the new drummer confirming the gig Thursday night. Looks like we're all set." He rubbed his hands together. "So, how are those steaks coming?"

After an impressive display of culinary skill, Ty served the steaks. Ashley stole a glance at his face but his expression was clear, the vulnerability she'd seen earlier replaced by his usual calm. If Rob noticed her preoccupation, he ignored it. He cut a piece off of his steak, and took a bite. "Damn, Ty this is amazing. What did you do?"

Ty acknowledged the compliment with a modest shrug. "It's all in the heat – you've got to get it high enough to sear but not burn." He shrugged. "I worked in a restaurant when I was in school."

Ashley pushed aside her distraction as a memory surfaced. "That's what you wanted to do after business school, wasn't it Ty? Open up a restaurant or club of some kind?"

"Something like that."

Rob snorted. "A bar in Oak Valley would hardly be a challenge for you, so I'm betting you had somewhere else in mind." Ty confirmed Rob's words with a nod. "What made you go back?" Rob asked.

"My father had a heart attack, and my folks needed me back in Oak Valley to run the family construction business. So I went back. That's when I met Ashley."

The softness in his voice made Ashley look up – and the heat on his face made her catch her breath. Rob looked between them. "How did you two meet?"

Ashley blushed. She remembered that summer. That day at the lake.

Rob noticed, of course, and chuckled. "What an interesting shade of red, Ashley. Now I've really gotta know."

Ty's lips curved into a sly smile. "I'd been back in town just a few days when my buddy Luke invited me to go out to the lake with a bunch of friends. Luke's sister Val brought along her new friend, Ashley. Her *hot* new friend, who was wearing this sexy little green bikini"

"I wasn't her new friend – I'd been in town for years." She turned to Rob. "I moved in with Granny after Ty left for college so we didn't meet until he returned."

Rob waved his hand. "I know all that – I want to get back to the bikini."

Ty smiled. "It was tiny – a few little triangles that hardly covered anything. She got up to go for a swim, and I followed, of course."

"Of course," Rob echoed.

Ty continued. "I passed her on the way to the floating dock and was already laying down on it when she caught up." Ty paused, his eyes distant with the memory. Ashley's thighs pressed together remembering what came next.

"She climbed up the ladder, water dripping from her hair and sliding down into her cleavage. The water was cold and her nipples hard, poking right through that top."

Rob whistled. "Damn, she must have looked hot."

Two sets of eyes dropped to Ashley's chest. Without looking down she knew her nipples were hard again, and visible through her tee. She crossed her arms. Rob laughed and turned back to Ty. "Go on."

"She paused on the ladder. Just stopped there, and was totally checking me out." He shook his head as if he still had trouble believing it. "Not subtly, either – her eyes started at my chest, and worked their way down. I swear she even licked her lips!"

Ashley couldn't believe she was sitting here listening to Ty talk to Rob about her. Even more incredible was how much it turned her on. Moisture flooded between her thighs, warm and wet, and a shiver passed over her skin. She stole sideways glances at the men. Ty's nostrils flared, and a muscle ticked in Rob's jaw as he swallowed. Clearly, she wasn't the only one affected by the story.

Ty spoke, his voice rougher than before. "By the time her eyes reached my cock, I was so hard, I thought I was going to come right there. I couldn't exactly hide the fact so I didn't bother trying." He turned to her, and his voice dropped another notch. "Remember what I asked you?"

Of course she did – he'd repeated his question last week. She nodded.

"Well?" Rob asked.

She looked down, and mumbled.

Rob leaned forward. "Sorry, Ash, I didn't catch that."

She repeated it louder. "See anything you like?"

Rob sat back, and looked at Ty with a grin. "And what did she say?"

Ty pushed back from the table, and pulled up his shirt to reveal taut abs. He traced the long, silver-white scar that arced down one side. "She asked me how I got this scar. Cool as a cucumber, like she hadn't been totally undressing me with her eyes."

Rob laughed. "Nice save, Ashley."

Ty laughed. "My thoughts exactly, but I wasn't going to let her off so easily. I followed her around the party until she agreed to come for a ride on my bike."

Rob nodded knowingly. "I bet you took her for some ride."
The two men laughed.

Holy shit. Were they really discussing the first time she and
Ty had sex? She looked down into her lap, and clenched her
hands to keep herself from squirming in her seat. Her heart was
racing. She had never gotten so hot, so fast.

Ty pushed his chair back, and got up from the table. Rob
rose too. Ashley looked from one man to the other, aroused but
not exactly sure of what was going on.

Ty spoke first. "So, Ashley... Want to go for a ride?" His
eyes shone with lust, and he held out his hand. Like he had that
night.

She glanced at Rob, and saw a similar look of desire on his
face. He nodded, and her breath caught in her chest.

They both wanted her. Here. Now. Together. And she
wanted them too, so badly her body was shaking. She needed to
feel them touching her, filling her, like a junkie needs a fix. She
nodded, and put her hand in Ty's. The other she offered to Rob,
and the two men pulled her to her feet.

Chapter Eighteen

Ty made an "after you" gesture. Ashley dropped the men's hands, and walked towards the bedrooms. Ty and Rob followed, their footsteps soft on the carpet. She hesitated a moment, then turned into her bedroom. Rob's bed was bigger, but she wanted the comfort and control of being on her own turf.

She stopped a few paces into the room. She'd led them this far, but she was unsure of what to do next. Climb onto the bed? Take off her clothes? She started to turn around when Ty stepped up behind her, and placed his hands on her waist. He turned them both so that she was facing the door, with him behind her. Rob stood by the doorway watching, his eyes half-lidded, rubbing his cock through his jeans.

From behind, Ty tugged off her shirt, then undid the catch on her bra. The lace cups fell away, exposing her breasts. "Isn't she beautiful?" Ty said. He took the swollen mounds in his hands, holding them up like offerings to Rob.

Rob nodded, and stepped forward. He brushed a kiss across her lips before leaning in to capture a nipple in his mouth. Ty rolled the other between his thumb and finger. She whimpered, pressing her ass back against Ty's hard cock.

Rob undid the fly of her jeans, and pushed them down to reveal her thong. He kneeled in front of her, and pressed his mouth against the lace triangle covering her mound. She could feel the warmth of his breath on her skin. She parted her legs to give him better access, and his tongue traced the seam of her lower lips. The material was rough against her swollen clit. She trembled. Ty rubbed his hands along her sides, down to her thighs and up again, kissing her neck and nipping at her ears.

After more torture, Rob pulled the thin material down her legs. She stepped out of the thong. He lifted one of her legs, and draped it over his shoulder. She leaned back against Ty for balance.

Ty glanced to the right. "Do you like what you see?" he asked.

Ashley followed his gaze. The three of them were reflected in the mirrored closet doors that covered one wall. Her face was flushed, lips swollen. Her bra still hung at her elbows, and her thong was pushed aside. Ty's fingers played with her nipples, and Rob's head was buried between her legs. She looked wanton. Passionate. Out of control.

Rob paused long enough to glance in the mirror. He smiled, then shifted his body so that her pussy was visible in the mirror, pink and glistening. He licked her again, slit to clit and back down, keeping his body angled so that she could watch each lick. His tongue danced over her sensitive flesh. Flicked against her clit. Thrust inside her wet channel. He sucked, and she fisted a hand in his hair.

She wasn't the only one who found the sight exciting – Ty groaned in her ear, and ground his cock against her ass. "Way too much clothing here," he said, and she nodded. Rob grabbed her hips to steady her, and Ty stepped back. He leaned back to pull off his shirt, then shucked his jeans. She watched his strip tease in the mirror. When he returned, the hot cock nestled between her butt cheeks was now bare smooth skin. She wriggled against him, and was rewarded with a growl.

Rob gave her one last long suck and stood. He wiped his mouth with the back of his hand but his lips and chin still gleamed with her juices. Ty walked them backwards until he was at the edge of the bed, and sat, pulling her onto his lap.

Rob licked his lips, and quickly shed his clothes. His cock stood out from his body, straining towards her. He kneeled, lifted her leg again, and hooked her thigh over Ty's. He did the same with her other leg. She was spread wipe open, completely exposed to both men – Rob in front of her and Ty through the reflection in the mirror. Ty's cock jutted out from between her legs. Ashley glanced at Rob. He stared at Ty's cock like a starving man at food.

Ty shifted her hips back, and positioned himself at her opening. "Okay, Ashley?"

Okay? She was far, far better than okay, but she nodded. Ty's hands tightened on her hips and he rocked her forward, thrusting upward. Slowly filling her.

Rob's lips parted. Their fucking was right at his eye-level. "Damn, that's hot," he said. He took his own cock in his fist. When Ty started pumping, Rob matched his rhythm. Ty's long pale cock was slipping in and out of her body, his balls swaying at its base. Rob leaned forward, and Ashley thought she was going to die when his tongue flicked against her clit. She remembered what he'd had said last night about fucking and sucking at the same time. Surely she had died and gone to heaven.

She looked in the mirror. Rob had angled himself again so that she could watch. His tongue laved her lips, and flicked against her clit, dangerously close to Ty's cock. Was he doing that on purpose? Did Ty know how close he was to having a man's lips on his cock? She looked at Ty's face in the mirror but he didn't meet her eyes. Instead his gaze was fixed on the point where their three bodies connected.

What would Ty do if Rob licked him? The thought alone made her hot. Suddenly she couldn't get the image out of her mind: these two beautiful men giving each other pleasure, getting each other off. A surge of heat rushed through her. Without letting herself reconsider, she shifted her hips up a fraction. Her movement took her out of the reach of Rob's mouth. It changed the angle of her joining with Ty just enough that his cock slipped out of her body. It sprang forward – onto Rob's open lips.

Rob didn't miss a beat. He took the tip of Ty's cock into his mouth, and sucked. His eyes were closed so Ashley couldn't tell what he was thinking. Her gaze flew to Ty's in the mirror but his eyes were also shut tight, his body arched against her as he cried out.

Ty kept pumping, and Rob held onto her thighs to take Ty's cock deeper into his mouth. Ashley shifted so that her slit bracketed Ty's cock and it slid between her lips with each thrust. Her clit bumped against Rob's lips, sending shock waves through her body.

She started to squirm – she wanted more. As if he'd heard her thoughts, Rob pulled his head back and Ty's cock slid out of his mouth. Rob grabbed it at the base, and guided it back into Ashley's body. Ty started pumping again, and Rob resumed lapping at her clit as if nothing had happened. As if he hadn't just been *sucking Ty's cock*.

Ty tilted her hips back a bit, and thrust. The angle was so

deep it hit some previously unfelt spot. Rob sucked hard at the same time, and Ashley went over the edge. A moment later Ty came too. Rob kept licking at her clit, drawing out her pleasure as Ty's movements slowed.

Ty lay back against the bed. Rob lifted her hips so Ty could move out from under her. She laid down again, and Ty slipped an arm around her, pulling her head onto his shoulder.

Rob came to kneel on the bed, but he wasn't done. The fingers of one hand played with her clit, sending aftershocks through her. His other hand gripped his cock, pumping it slowly while he looked at her and Ty with lust in his eyes.

She felt her body stir. She'd just experienced a mind- and body-shattering orgasm – could she be ready for another one already? Watching Rob's hand and feeling his fingers, she thought she might.

"Ashley." Rob's voice sent chills up her spine, and made her womb clench. She looked over at Ty. His eyes were closed, and a lazy smile played over his lips. His fingers drew circles on her shoulder.

Rob looked down at her wet slit, which glistened with Ty's cum and his own saliva. A muscle ticked in his jaw. He looked up at her face. She nodded. He knelt between her thighs. She reached down, and wrapped her hand around his as he guided his cock into her slit. When he was fully seated he closed his eyes then stretched out on top of her. His chest pressed against hers, weight resting on his forearms. He dropped his head alongside hers, still not moving within, and breathed into her ear. "Oh God, Ash."

Her hand came up to rest on the back of his head. She clenched her inner muscles around him, and wriggled. He felt so good inside her.

Rob came up on his elbows, and took her mouth in a deep kiss. She could taste her juices on his tongue – and maybe even Ty's. In her mind's eye, she saw his lips around Ty's cock, and her arousal climbed another notch. It was hot when the two of them touched, and pleasured her. When they also did it to each other? *Damn.*

Rob propped himself up on his elbows and started to pump. Slow at first, then faster and faster. She had come but already she could feel another orgasm building.

Rob's cock felt totally different from Ty's but just as good. How had she ever thought that she could choose between these two men?

Rob pushed up onto his hands, deepening the angle of his thrusts. Ty leaned over, and took her nipple between his teeth. Rob thrust, and Ty nipped, sending a spark of exquisite pain and pleasure shooting from her breast to her clit and back. She exploded, her inner muscles clenching at Rob's cock. He threw his head back, and cried out. She could feel his cock pulsing as a shot of warmth spilled into her.

Two men. Twice the pleasure and the thrill of watching them with each other. It didn't get any better than that.

Chapter Nineteen

Ty woke in a tangle of limbs. It took him a moment to get his bearings. A soft body curved in front of him, warming him from chest to thigh. His arm stretched across the pillow, and his fingers entwined in soft silky hair. Short, straight hair. Rob's hair.

Ty had expressed in sleep what his conscious mind had denied. His first thought was to pull back but he stopped. It felt good to touch Rob. And damned good when the other man touched him. *Sucked* him. Ty's cock stirred. Fuck, that had felt good.

So, what did it mean? When Matt had come onto him, he'd turned the other guy down because he knew he wasn't gay. Knew he liked women. Now Ty wondered if he'd dismissed his curiosity too quickly.

Ashley stirred against him, and rolled onto her stomach. Ty's hand fell away from Rob's head, as the other man opened his eyes. Had he felt Ty's touch?

Rob rubbed a hand over Ashley's hair. "Morning gorgeous." She groaned, and pulled a pillow over her head. Rob laughed and looked at Ty. "I think someone needs coffee."

A muffled "umm hmm" came from under the pillow. Rob

hopped out of bed, and headed for the door, still naked. Ty checked out his rear view until the other man disappeared down the hall.

He looked down. Ashley had pulled the pillow off her head and was looking at him with a curious expression. He waited for the interrogation, but none came, so he got up, and retrieved his boxers from the floor.

Ashley pulled herself out of bed, and into a pair of yoga pants and a tee. She looked so deliciously sexy that Ty had to resist the urge to tumble her back into bed. Instead he followed her into the kitchen.

Rob was dressed in sweats, and stood in front of the fridge. "Ash, I have bad news. We're out of milk."

Ashley gave a gasp of outrage. Ty suspected that she was only half joking – the woman really needed her coffee.

Rob held up his hands, and laughed. "Calm down, girl. I'll run out and get some." He grabbed his wallet and keys, and left.

The door closed. Ty took a breath and turned to Ashley. "Rob is bi." He'd meant for it to come out as a question, but as soon as the statement left his lips, he knew it was true.

Ash stopped her coffee prep, and looked up. Her expression was cautious, and she gave a slow nod.

"That explains a lot." He shook his head with a laugh. "It's kind of funny. The night we met at Granny's I thought he was homophobic. Something he said when I mentioned Matt. He mostly goes for women though, right?"

She shook her head. "Men. In fact in the whole time I've known him, Rob has *only* been with men."

"Really?" She nodded. "Interesting." He paused then cleared his throat. "Remember how I told you that Rob reminded me of Matt?"

"The guy you played football with? Yeah..." Ashley stopped in mid-sentence, and realization dawned on her face. "Now I remember why Matt's name sounded familiar. He's gay, isn't he? Came out of the closet after he got injured."

Ty snorted. "He was forced out of the closet, but yes, Matt is gay."

"Did you know that at the time? When you two were playing ball together?"

"Sort of. I mean, I didn't really know what it meant." She looked confused so he elaborated. "He wasn't sure himself. Oak Valley isn't exactly an easy place to explore things like that. But I knew that he was curious."

"He told you no, he didn't tell you. He hit on you, didn't he?"

Ty nodded.

"And?"

Ty shrugged. "I told him I wasn't interested. I mean I wasn't offended. Well, not for long. I figured out that it was a compliment of sorts."

She let out her breath slowly. "Did you ever regret it? Not taking Matt up on his... interest? Were you ever curious about what it would have been like?"

The click of the doorknob saved Ty from having to reply. He turned towards the door. Rob stepped in, a plastic bag in one hand, and a stack of mail in the other. "I'm back." He looked slowly between Ty and Ashley. "Anything exciting happen while I was gone?"

Rob's tone was casual, but Ty knew that those brown eyes missed nothing. Ashley shook her head. "I was about to make that coffee. I don't think I can survive another minute caffeine-free."

Rob's brows went up. "I'm surprised you didn't get it going while I was out."

Ashley darted a glance at Ty. "I was going to but–"

"But I distracted her." He turned back to Ashley. "And to answer your question, I have no regrets." He tossed a glance over at Rob, and smiled. "Not anymore."

No regrets? What had they been talking about while he was out? Ashley looked a bit shell-shocked, but Ty was smiling so Rob wasn't worried. Just really, *really*, curious.

Ashley grabbed the milk, and headed into the kitchen. Rob followed, measuring the water while she took out the beans. She hummed to herself as she did so. The tune sounded familiar. Rob put a hand on her arm. "What's that?"

She looked down at the coffee things on the counter. "What's what?"

"Not the coffee, Ash – the tune you're humming."

She seemed to think about it for a moment then shook her head. "Don't know. Woke up humming it."

He waved his hand impatiently. "Hum it again." She did. He clapped his hands together. "Yes! That's the tune I played for you last week. The one I was thinking about to go with the song you were working, "Making It Real."

She nodded. "That's right. It sounded familiar. It's been going through my head since I woke up but I couldn't remember where I'd heard it. It's catchy."

Rob shook his head. "Not the way I wrote it. I had: *da da da dat da da* for the bridge but that's not what you were humming. I like your version better. I knew there was something wrong, but couldn't figure out where to go with it." Rob grabbed Ashley's shoulders, and planted a firm kiss on her lips. "Ash, you're brilliant."

He dashed out of the kitchen. Ty gave him a look of surprise as he hurried past, but Rob shook his head. A moment later he returned to the living room with his favorite guitar, the battered acoustic he'd brought to Nashville eight years ago. Ashley had already retrieved her guitar from its resting place beside the bookcase. She waited on the end of the couch.

Ty looked between them. "It looks like you guys have work to do so I'll be going." He reached for his jacket.

Without thinking Rob held up a hand. "Don't go." Ty stopped, and Rob cleared his throat. "I mean you don't have to go. We're cool with having an audience, right Ash? If you want to stay and listen, that is."

Ashley nodded. "That would be great." She turned to Rob. "Remember the song I was playing at the fair the night we met? Ty helped me with that one."

Rob smiled. "Great then, it's decided. You give us feedback on the song, and we'll comp you a pass for the show." Rob thought about what they'd done last night, the feel of the other man's cock between his lips. He'd offer Ty a whole lot more if he thought the other man would be interested.

Ty laughed. "Sounds like a deal."

Pushing his desire aside for the moment, Rob began strumming. Ashley joined in. When they reached the bridge, they substituted the change she'd made. Perfect. He pulled out a notebook and started jotting down notes. "Ash, once again your overnight imagination has solved our problems."

An hour and a half later Ashley sat back, pulling the guitar strap over her head. They'd worked out most of the song, and fine-tuned the lyrics. Ty had contributed too, giving feedback and even helping out when they got stuck. He had a great ear and seemed to know something about music. Rob shot him a look out of the corner of his eye. What other secrets was the man hiding?

Rob noticed Ashley looking at him quizzically, and smiled. "This song is going to be great, Ash. You know, it reminds me a bit of that song you were working on last year, 'Knowing Home.'"

She gave a wry smile, and turned to Ty. "The label didn't want to record that one. Said it was too *edgy*." She made quotes around the word. "Not pop enough for them."

Rob shook his head, frustrated. "Those jerks don't know crap about music. They're just looking for a product to sell. They all say they want the next big thing, the next sound, but no one is willing to stick out their necks out to make it happen."

Ty nodded. "But when someone else does, you can bet they'll jump on the bandwagon and try to produce five more acts that sound just like it."

Rob pointed at him, and nodded. "Exactly. All the more reason to go indie now, and make something interesting happen on our own." He shook the notebook. "Let the labels try to imitate us when we've hit it big with this. And that edgy song. I'm telling you Ash..."

She held up her hands as if to ward him off. "I know, I know. Other folks have made it as indie acts. But it's so much work – writing, playing, recording, producing, distributing, not to mention publicity and building a fan base. How do they do it all?"

"They don't," Ty said. "They put together a good team. Hire others to do it for them–"

Rob nodded vigorously. "–Instead of blindly trusting the label to do it. Hell, Ash we do most of that stuff ourselves anyway. Promo. Songwriting. Why not cut ties, and stop paying them a share for the privilege of putting up with their bullshit?"

"You make it sound so easy, but…"

"It's not easy." Ty said, and Ashley shot Rob a smug look. Ty continued. "But getting to this point wasn't easy, either. Was it?"

Ashley conceded the point, and narrowed her eyes at Ty. "So you're an expert on the music biz now?"

Ty gave a small shrug. "At some level, business is business."

Ashley looked uneasy. Rob knew she found the prospect of going it alone daunting, and felt more comfortable relying on "professionals" like Brad. If she only knew   no, he'd keep Brad's criticism to himself. He wanted a partner who was enthusiastic about becoming an independent artist, not one who felt like she'd been backed into a corner.

Ash looked between the two men and shrugged. "Let me think about it, okay?"

Rob bit back a frustrated sigh, and nodded. Ash would come around to the indie idea at her own pace or not at all.

Chapter Twenty

Ty settled behind his oak desk, and pulled an accordion folder from his briefcase. He'd taken this office in Nashville some months ago in anticipation of getting more involved in the club, but hadn't used it much. Now he was grateful to have it – if he was going to spend more time with Ashley and Rob, it would be convenient to have an office in town.

Should he have told them about his involvement in the club? He shook his head. It would be his little surprise. A way to show Ashley how he really felt. If he could get them in, Sweet Talk would be a great addition to the show, and success at the opening could give them the boost they needed to either get a recording deal or build momentum for an indie career. A win-win for everyone.

He opened the folder. Where was that list? The club manager had provided all the investors with a thick folder that included construction details, scheduling procedures, and staffing but he hadn't looked at it beyond a cursory glance.

He riffled through the pages until he found what he was looking for: Roadhouse Key Personnel. He pulled out the stapled stack of papers, and scanned the list until he found the title he wanted: *Venue Promoter - Jolene McCreary*. The woman responsible for booking acts for the Roadhouse, including for the opening night.

He dialed Jolene's number and waited for someone to pick up.

"Hello, this is the Roadhouse, Nashville's newest and hottest music venue. How may I help you?"

Ty introduced himself, and the man who answered the phone promised to connect him to Jolene. The woman herself came on a moment later.

"Hello. This is Jolene McCreary. How may I help you, sir?

"Hello Jolene. My name is Tyler Monroe. I'm one of the investors in the Roadhouse."

"I know your name, sir. It's on the program."

"Of course." He'd forgotten about how visible his role would be. Yes, it would be best to tell Ashley and Rob sooner rather than later. He was going to their gig tonight – he'd mention it then.

"Jolene, I was calling to talk to you about the acts that have been booked for the show so far."

"I've finished updating the list – I could send it over if you like. We just got confirmations from Ace in the Hole and from the Townies, and the Jack Lawn Band is trying to juggle their travel schedule so they can be there."

Ty could hear the pride filling Jolene's voice. "And the smaller acts that are going to fill the gap left by the cancelation? Have you identified them yet?'

"All but one. Do you have a suggestion?"

"Yes. Are you familiar with the band Sweet Talk?"

"Ashley Ford and Rob Porter? Oh yes. Saw them downtown last year, and loved them."

Ty could hear papers shuffling. "Funny you mention them, Mr. Monroe. I received a call from their manager yesterday, proposing Rob Porter as a solo act. I didn't know Porter performed alone, and wanted to run it by the creative team before I gave him an answer."

A chill stole over Ty. *Rob performing solo?* It wasn't unheard of for the members of an act to also have solo careers, but Ty hadn't heard Rob or Ashley mention it. And when they'd discussed their plans earlier, Rob hadn't said anything about going at it alone. "I didn't know he did either."

"Maybe Miss Ford wasn't available?"

The Ashley Ford he knew would cancel Christmas to be a part of the club opening. No, he was pretty sure Ashley had no idea of what Rob was planning. He pushed that thought aside for the moment. "I don't know about Porter's solo ambitions, but I'd like to see Sweet Talk up there as a duo. Can you contact their manager and see if they're available?"

"Of course, Mr. Monroe. I'll let you know what he says."

"Thanks. And Jolene, I would appreciate it if you didn't mention that I was the one who requested them."

Jolene agreed to keep his name out of it, and signed off.

Ty sat back in his chair, and stared out the window. Rob was frustrated with Ashley's reluctance to go indie, but he'd also been vocal in praise of her talent, crediting her with fixing their latest song. He'd sounded sincere, but was he truly committed to Ashley – or was his "loyalty" a cover for a guilty conscience?

Damn. He'd started to like Rob – or at least the person he *thought* Rob was. With everything they'd shared yesterday – dinner, sex, Ashley – Ty had started to wonder if maybe there could be more to their relationship. And after the conversation he'd had with Ashley...

He took a deep breath, and thought for a moment. Could there be a reasonable explanation for Rob's actions? Ty tried, but he couldn't think of any.

His own conscience gave a twinge, and he grimaced. Rob wasn't the only one with secrets. All the more reason for Ty to come clean about his involvement with the Roadhouse. Before Ashley found out from someone else. He'd tell her after their gig tonight.

Right after he got the truth out of Rob Porter.

The stage lights flickered off signaling the end of the last set. Ashley sat back on her stool, and closed her eyes. Her spirit slowly settled back onto her bones. She smiled at the familiar feeling. Before her slump, performing had always affected her like this. She didn't want to jinx herself, but it seemed like a good sign.

She picked up her guitar, and made her way to the edge of the stage where Rob was waiting, a big smile on his face. They'd performed two sets and three encores, and when the crowd had called for more Rob had let them know about Sweet Talk's next performance. At the Roadhouse's opening night gala.

Rob grabbed her around the waist, and pulled her into a hug. "We were great, Ash. They couldn't get enough."

She laughed against his shoulder. "I know. For a moment I was afraid you were going to insist on a fourth encore – and a second kiss."

"Another kiss I'd take, but no more music. Got to leave 'em wanting more. Then they'll buy tickets to see us at the

Roadhouse next month." He pulled back, and looked at her. "Ashley, we're playing at the opening. We're going to be on stage with the biggest names in country music."

Brad had sprung the news on them right before the show. It had totally pumped them up. "I know," she said. "I still can't believe it."

"Believe it, babe. 'cause it's true. Didn't I tell you it would all work out?" He shook her shoulders lightly, and she nodded. "Then I don't want to hear any more talk about bad reviews or slumps – all that's behind us. It's only going to get better from here. You'll see."

She leaned into Rob's chest for another hug. What would she have done without his faith and optimism to keep her going these past few weeks?

He pulled back and gave her a quick kiss on the lips. "Time to go greet our adoring fans, beautiful." With an arm slung over her shoulder, he turned them back towards the room.

As soon as they stepped off the stage, people crowded around. Brad was alongside them in a heartbeat, handing out postcards for Rob and Ashley to sign, and directing fans to their website and Facebook page. Spots danced before her eyes from all the people snapping pictures on their phones.

She looked over to the corner where Ty had been sitting. His seat was empty, but she knew he was around here somewhere. Probably hanging back until the fans were done. She'd spotted him as soon as she came onstage. He'd grabbed a seat outside of the glare of the lights knowing that she'd be able to see him that way, a trick he'd learned years ago when she'd played at Charley's. Seeing him there during the show had wiped out any trace of nerves, and when singing the love songs she'd had to force herself to look around, and not sing only to him.

They'd come full circle. It was like the past three years had never happened. Like that fight had never pushed them apart. He was obviously supportive of her music now so she figured it was time to put that night firmly in the past, and let the future determine where her relationship with Ty – and Rob – would go.

Rob pulled her close for another picture, and she smiled. How lucky was she to have both of these men in her life? With Rob singing beside her, and Ty encouraging her from the audience she'd felt invincible. And it had really shown in her performance.

After extracting a promise that Sweet Talk would be back at the bar next week, the last few fans went to get drinks. Rob pulled his shirt away from his chest. "Damn, I'm hot. I'm going to step outside to cool off for a few minutes."

"I'll go look for Ty. I can't wait to tell him about opening night at Roadhouse!"

Rob nodded. "He'll be psyched for us. We have to be sure to get him a comp ticket."

"Definitely. I want him to be there."

Rob smiled. "Me too." He turned down the hall, and waved over his shoulder. "See you in a few."

Ashley wove her way through the room, stopping every few feet to chat with friends and fans. She searched the crowd for Ty, finally locating him by the bar. A fan stopped her for an autograph a few tables short of her destination, and she smiled at Ty with a shrug. He nodded. He had his poker face on, which Ashley now recognized as the expression he wore when he was uncomfortable or upset. She'd have expected him to be happy about their performance. Had he seen something from the audience that they'd missed?

She was being ridiculous. Ty wasn't involved in Sweet Talk the way she and Rob were. Why should his mood rise and fall with their performances? After the interest he'd shown when she and Rob had practiced this morning, it was easy to forget that he had a life outside of country music. He was probably preoccupied with something that had happened with his business. She'd ask him about it later, when the three of them were alone.

She finally made her way to Ty's side. His expression softened, and he kissed her on the top of the head, his hands on her hips. She leaned towards him for more, but his grip held her back. She sighed. He was right, of course. After seeing her and Rob onstage, what would people think if she kissed Ty? Their unusual relationship was not one she was ready to explain to strangers.

She stepped back, and looked at him, letting every lewd thought she was having show on her face. He blinked as if surprised. She was gratified to see a smile crack his lips.

"You were amazing, Ashley. Really great."

"Thanks. Seeing you in the audience really made a difference. It was like old times. Hey, we have big news. Brad got a call from the venue promoter at the Roadhouse, a new place that's opening downtown. Sweet Talk has been invited to perform opening night."

"That's great, Ashley. Congratulations." He didn't seem as excited as she'd expected. Then again, he had no way of knowing what an opportunity this would be for them.

"I still can't believe it. There will be some really big names up there."

"And you deserve to be one of them. You've worked hard

for this."

"We have, haven't we? But after the hard time I'd been having, this is so validating, you know?" She shook her head. "Rob kept telling me that my slump wouldn't last but I never expected this kind of comeback."

He gave a small smile. "So where is Rob?"

Ashley pointed over her shoulder to the back hall. "He stepped outside to cool off."

"Excuse me for a sec, Ashley. I want to ask Rob something."

Chapter Twenty-One

After another round of congratulations and drinks, Ashley looked around. Rob and Ty still hadn't returned. Were they outside? She smiled. Maybe they'd taken advantage of the moment alone to have a quick smooch in the alley. Wouldn't it be fun to walk in on *that*? Sure it was unlikely, but a girl could dream. Then again, was it only a dream? Rob was obviously attracted to Ty, and Ty seemed to be at least curious about Rob.

She retrieved her purse from behind the bar, and headed to the bathroom to freshen up. Beyond the ladies room, someone had propped open the exit door, presumably to let in some air. She thought she heard male voices coming from outside, arguing, but with the music playing in the background it was hard to hear what was being said.

Ashley poked her head through the door. Rob and Ty stood ten feet away, facing one another. Their bodies were as tense as gunslingers preparing for a fight with hostile expressions to match. She was about to announce her presence when Rob's voice carried to her loud and clear.

"I put myself forward as a solo act for the opening night at the Roadhouse."

Ashley's heart leaped into her throat, and she froze. *What?*

She must have spoken aloud because both men whirled to face her. Rob's expression showed surprise while Ty's held determination and anger. She turned to Rob. "Did I just hear you say that you put yourself forward as a solo act for the Roadhouse?"

"Yes. I mean no." He took a deep breath. "That's what I said. But I'm as surprised to hear it as you are."

She into the alley. "How could you be surprised? Either you did or you didn't."

"I didn't. I swear. But he," Rob jerked his head in Ty's direction, "seems to think that I did."

Ashley turned to Ty. He lifted his chin. "That's what I was told. I was just asking Rob about it."

"Accusing me is more like it." Rob's hands curled into fists.

Ty didn't back down. "I wanted to know how your name came up as a possible solo act."

"I have no idea," Rob said on a snarl. He turned to Ashley with a pleading look in his eye. "Ashley, I swear I have never considered performing without you."

She wanted to believe him, but doubt curled in her gut. "Not even when, you know, I was –."

Anger flashed in Rob's eyes. "Never."

She narrowed her eyes. "Then who suggested it?"

Ty's expression turned thoughtful. "Isn't your agent responsible for booking gigs?"

Rob shook his head. "That bastard. Brad kept talking about those bad reviews, and said that we could take the pressure off you, but I never thought he would go this far."

Ashley's mouth opened in shock. The nasty surprises kept coming. "Brad said what?"

A guilty look crossed Rob's face, one she'd seen before. *What the hell?*

He held up his hands in a placating posture. "He cornered me when you were out of town. And again the other day, after practice. I knew he was wrong, Ashley, so I didn't say anything to you. I didn't want you to—"

"Collapse into a self-pitying blob of Jell-O? Cry myself to sleep? How dare you treat me like that? I'm a professional Rob, and I deserve to know what the man I'm paying says about me behind my back."

She took a deep breath, and tried to control her racing heartbeat when something else occurred to her. She turned to Ty. "How did *you* know about this anyway?"

Rob's eyes narrowed. "Good question."

Ty opened his mouth, and closed it, then swallowed. He looked more uncomfortable than she'd ever seen him. "I spoke to the venue promoter at the Roadhouse."

Ashley jerked back in surprise. "The venue promoter? But why would they tell you? I mean that's not the kind of info they give to the public."

Rob's eyes went wide, and he pointed an accusing finger at Ty. "That's it. The project you invested in. It's the Roadhouse, isn't it?"

Looking like he'd rather be anywhere else, Ty nodded. Ashley's jaw dropped. "You're an investor in the Roadhouse?" She shook her head as another realization came to her. "You're the reason Sweet Talk was invited to play. It wasn't because my performances have improved – it's because you felt *sorry* for me." She pointed back at the door she'd come through. "You let me go on like an idiot about how validating it was to be invited when *you* were the only reason we got a slot."

Ty spread his hands before him. "It wasn't like that, Ashley. I wanted to help I mean, in business people do favors for each other all the time."

Ashley inhaled sharply. "Don't you dare patronize me, Tyler Monroe. As if I don't know how this business works." She put her hands on her hips. "If this was *that* kind of favor, why didn't you tell me upfront? Why keep your role in the club a secret from us this whole time?"

Ty opened his mouth to speak but nothing came out.

Convenient time for him to be at a loss for words. "Just as I thought. You can keep your damned lectures about how the real world works to yourself." She shook her head. "Nothing's changed. Three years later and you still don't think I have what it takes to make it on my own."

Ty looked surprised. "What are you talking about? I never said that."

The pain of that betrayal came rushing back, as raw as if it had happened only moments ago. "No? The night I told you about Rob's offer, all you could come up with were reasons why I shouldn't go. Why it wouldn't work." She fought to keep her voice steady but it came out as a sob. "Damn you, Tyler Monroe."

Rob took a step forward, but she raised a hand before he could touch her. "Damn you too, Rob Porter. I trusted you." She looked at both men. "I trusted you both, and believed in…" she waved her hands to encompass the three of them "whatever the hell this thing was that we were doing together." Tears blurred the scene before her. "And I thought you two believed in me."

She pivoted on her heel, and bolted for the fire door.

"Ashley, wait!" someone called from behind her but she kept going, stumbling over the threshold, and into the back hall. She slipped sideways through the crowd until she reached the front door.

Neon lights and music poured onto the sidewalks on both sides of the street, and clusters of people wandered from one club to the next. Head down, she wove between them biting her lip to hold back the flood. The last thing she wanted was for a fan or reporter to see her like this.

She turned down the first side street. Then the next. She kept walking, until the noise of the main drag faded, and all she could here were the click clicking of her boots accompanied by the sound of blood pounding in her ears.

Chapter Twenty-Two

Where the hell were her keys? Ashley squinted into her bag. The sunglasses protecting her swollen eyes from the morning's glare cast the interior of her bag into darkness, so she couldn't find a thing.

She'd crashed at a friend's place and woken up with a crying hangover: an aching head, puffy red eyes, and a killer sore throat. Makeup had taken care of the worst external effects, but hadn't done a thing for the heaviness she felt inside.

Her friend had invited Ashley to spend the day at her place, but Ashley had opted to come home. After stewing over what she'd heard last night, she was itching to confront somebody.

With a frustrated growl, she yanked her makeup bag aside. The small pouch caught on the purse's zipper, upending the larger bag's contents all over the welcome mat. Lipstick, tissues, aspirin, and dozens of other essentials spilled over her boots. Her keys landed with a noisy jangle on her foot. She crouched down, tottering on tired feet, and her keys disappeared in another blur of tears.

She'd had enough. Up-and-down performances. An elusive recording deal. A damned two-faced agent. On top of all that she'd gotten involved in God-knows-what with not one but *two* men. Men who kept secrets. Men who couldn't be trusted.

Enough. The emotional roller coaster had taken one too many dips. She was getting off. But first she had to get inside. She started to gather her scattered things, and the door opened. Jeans-clad legs stood before her, ending in a familiar pair of bare feet. Long and pale, they somehow looked vulnerable and a wee bit sexy. She closed her eyes. How brainwashed was she that Rob's *feet* looked sexy? Surely that was a sign that she needed to disentangle herself from this relationship, and fast.

"Ashley?"

She kept her eyes on the mat. He crouched down, and reached out to help her pick things up but she pushed his hand away. She didn't want his help, didn't want him so close she could smell his aftershave, and *certainly* didn't want his bare, shower-damp chest within her field of vision.

From the corner of her eye she saw him shake his head. He brushed her hand aside, and picked up a comb and her nail file. *Fine.* He could do the cleaning up. She stood, wobbled for a moment, then slipped past him into the apartment. Rob sighed behind her.

She stopped in the middle of the room, and dropped her head into her hands. She was being childish – she knew that. But she was so angry and confused and hurt, and had absolutely no idea of what to do with those feelings. Why had she come home again?

The door snicked shut. Footsteps sounded on the carpet behind her. "Ashley, I'm sorry."

Her heart twisted at the pain in his voice, and she looked down at her feet. Maybe now wasn't a good time for confrontation. What she needed was distance. Time to think.

She took a step towards her bedroom.

Rob came up behind her. "Talk to me. Please." He laid a hand on her shoulder, as if he were afraid she would bolt. "Don't run away."

Run away? Hadn't Ty accused her of doing the same thing? She looked down the hallway, towards her bedroom. What was she going to do anyway – lock herself in? It wasn't like Rob hadn't invaded the room a hundred times. His imprint was all over the place, his smell on the sheets. Besides, there were things to be said, answers she needed to hear. No, she wouldn't run this time. She would stand her ground, and fight.

She spun out of Rob's grip and faced him, hands on her hips. "Yes, we have to talk."

Relief washed over Rob's face. He gestured towards the couch. She shook her head. Standing her ground was easier on two feet.

"Ash, those boots have got to be killing you by now. At least take them off."

As if conjured by his words, a sharp pain stabbed the ball of her right foot. She shifted from one foot to the other, then perched on the edge of the couch. As soon as the boots were off, she stood again.

Rob gestured toward the kitchen. "Want anything? I made you some coffee." She shook her head, and he sighed. "Ashley, I don't want to fight with you. I want to talk."

It was hard to stay angry at someone who sounded as forlorn as Rob did at that moment. The fight started to drain out of her like water from a tub. Then she thought of her mother. *Had Mama's man troubles started like this? Was that how she'd lost her focus and drive?*

Ashley forced herself to remain strong, and wrapped her

indignation around her like a cloak. Still, coffee would be nice. She nodded, and sat down. "Yes. Coffee. Please."

Rob hustled into the kitchen, returning with her favorite mug filled to the brim. He handed it to her, then took a step back and spread his hands wide. "Look Ash, I'm sorry. I'm sorry I didn't tell you what Brad said. I'm sorry if it seemed like I was coddling you. It's... well, you had a lot going on, and I didn't think that hearing Brad's B.S. was going to make it easier."

Nothing like laying it all out there. She put down the cup, and crossed her arms. "You were patronizing me."

Rob's back stiffened. "I was trying to protect you. There's a difference."

He didn't get it. She shook her head. "I'm a professional, Rob. I need to know when things are bad. In the past, if I was playing badly you'd tell me, not try to protect my feelings. You used to trust me. "

"I know. Things seemed different lately. *You* seemed different. More stressed. Like your performing wasn't the only thing bothering you. I figured that when the other stuff cleared up, the playing would bounce back."

What he was saying rang true on some level. It *hadn't* just been the playing. It'd been their relationship, the attraction that she'd had for him that kept getting stronger. But her music had fallen apart before all that, hadn't it? Still she had to give credit where it was due. She pinched the bridge of her nose. "You're right. There was more going on. I just hate the idea of everyone thinking that I can't handle it. *You* thinking that."

Rob crouched before her, and put his hands on her arms. "No one thought you couldn't handle it. Forget about Brad," he said when she opened her mouth to protest. "His contract is done, and we don't need someone like that." He shook her arms lightly. "I wasn't worried about the music or your performance. I was worried about *you*, Ashley. I didn't mean to hide anything from you, I swear."

She frowned. "Unlike Ty."

Rob shrugged, and the anger that had dissipated earlier bubbled up in her again. Rob's actions were understandable, but Ty had deliberately kept things from them. That would be harder to explain – or forgive.

Rob inhaled slowly. "Speaking of that... Maybe we should talk to him before jumping to conclusions. You never know—"

She gave an exasperated huff. "He lied to us, Rob – by omission if not directly. What I can't figure out is why."

"Maybe it didn't come up? There wasn't a good opportunity?"

"You mean between the fucking and the sucking he never got the chance to mention that he's an investor in the hottest club to open in Nashville in a decade? Somehow I find that hard to believe."

Rob sat back on his heels. "Don't you think you're being a bit harsh, Ash? You know him better than I do but"

"You're right, I do – and I should have known better. The man always knew how to get under my defenses." She shook her head. "How could I have been so stupid?"

He laid a hand on her arm. "Ash, calm down. I honestly think he meant well, even if he didn't go about it in the best way."

Ashley shook off Rob's hand, stood up, and paced away from the couch. She knew that Rob was attracted to Ty, but what if he had started to feel more than just lust? Could his feelings for the other man blind him to Ty's flaws? She whirled back to face him. "You're making excuses for him. You want to believe he's a good guy because you like having him around."

"That's not true."

Ashley didn't let him finish. "You don't care about what he's done to me – now or in the past. You just want to get him in bed."

Rob sucked in a breath, and a muscle ticked in his jaw. "Is that what you really think of me, Ash? That I would toss away everything we have – professionally and personally – for a piece of ass?"

Is that really what I think? Or is jealousy making me crazy?

Ashley shook her head. *Why would I be jealous of Rob and Ty?* The answer shocked her with its clarity. She was jealous of Rob's interest in Ty and vice versa, because *her* feelings for both men were a lot deeper than she'd ever allowed herself to acknowledge. As deep as they get.

When the hell had that happened?

Rob stepped right up in her face, so close she could feel the anger radiating off his body. "Well, is it?" he asked.

She couldn't speak. She shook her head, and tried to retreat. She had to get away, to escape before he realized what she was thinking. She stepped back, and he followed.

She looked in his face; she could read the warning there but kept going, prodded on by her own confusion and pain. "Well, that's what this is all about, isn't it? I'm just an accessory, a way to help you get together with Ty."

"You are not an accessory, Ash." His voice came out on a growl. "I thought I proved that the other night when we were alone in bed."

Heat flared in her gut as she recalled his delicious assault on her ass. She tried to push the feelings aside, lashing out as she did so. "That was an exception. You like men, remember?"

"Ash, I told you that I like women too – I've *always* liked women. You chose to ignore that."

"No, I chose to pay attention to the evidence in front of me, which was you trolling gay bars, and coming home to rub your latest conquest in my face."

Rob was silent, his mouth open. Even Ashley was surprised by the venom in her voice. He shook his head. "Ashley. I never meant to flaunt my… what I was doing. I'm sorry if it came across that way."

His voice was soft and full of apology. She rubbed a hand over her face. "I know – forget I said that. The point is, in all the time that I've known you, you've only ever slept with guys."

He pulled her into his arms. "That's because I was already in love with a woman, Ash. You."

Her heart jumped and lodged in her throat. *What did he said?*

He pulled back, and looked in her eyes. "I love you Ash. I have for a long time. But you were so closed off, that I pushed those feelings down, hiding them even from myself. Since you weren't available, I had casual sex with guys, and tried to convince myself that that was all I needed."

Ashley remembered how to breathe, and blinked up at Rob. "You… you really love me? Like as in happily-ever-after kind of love?"

His answer was a kiss that made her light-headed and tingly from her scalp to her toes. Then, he gathered her to his chest, and kissed the top of her head. "Yes, Ashley, I do. And I know we can make this work."

It sounded good but something was still missing. She looked at Rob. "But what about men? You said you liked both – could you live with only having one?"

He nodded, but Ashley thought she saw a flicker of

uncertainty in his eyes. "Of course, Ashley. You are more than enough for me."

Was that true – and was it true for her too? Yes, she loved Rob, but if she was being honest with herself, she loved Ty too, and had for years. And from what both men had told her, they were interested in one another too.

An image flashed into her head of Rob sucking Ty's cock as it pumped between her thighs. Was that what Rob needed – a woman *and* a man? In spite of what he'd said about having casual sex with men because she was unavailable, he seemed to enjoy having Ty around.

Maybe she should try to give Ty the benefit of the doubt. For Rob's sake.

And perhaps for her own as well.

Ashley settled on the couch with her coffee "What happened after I left last night?"

Rob sat next to her with a shrug. "Nothing else happened between Ty and me, if that's what you're asking. We went after you, but by the time we got outside, you were gone. Then Ty took off. I'm surprised you haven't heard from him."

Ashley got out, and grabbed her bag. "He may have tried - I turned my phone off after I left the bar." She retrieved her phone, and powered it on. It gave a chirp - she had messages. "Ty called, and texted me last night and this morning. And I have four - no five – messages from Brad. I wonder what that's about."

Rob nodded. "Brad left messages for me too, but I haven't contacted him yet. I wanted to talk to you first."

Ashley sank back onto the couch. "Right - we have to deal with Brad."

"Brad can wait - let's worry about Ty first."

"You are worried about Ty, aren't you?"

Rob nodded.

"Okay, I'll talk him." She thumbed a text into her phone. "I told him that we're home and he should come by."

A few minutes later a knock sounded on the door. Rob got up to answer it. "I bet I know who that is."

Ashley stood up, wiping her palms on last night's jeans, and Rob opened the door. Ty stood in the doorway. His shirt was rumpled, and his eyes were ringed with shadows. His usually neat black hair stood up in front as if he'd been running his hands through it.

He stepped towards her with his hands out. "Ashley. I'm sorry."

Rob pointed a thumb towards the hall. "I'll, um, leave you two alone."

Ashley held up a hand. "Stay. I think we all need to talk." She raised a brow in Ty's direction, and he nodded. She returned to the couch. Rob sat beside her.

Ty took the chair across from them. He shook his head. "I'm sorry that I didn't tell you about my involvement with the Roadhouse sooner. The truth is that I didn't know how to tell you. Shortly after you left town, a business school friend approached me with the opportunity to invest in a new Nashville club. I jumped at the chance." He shook his head, and looked down at his hands. "The numbers looked good, and the project sounded like fun, but that wasn't why I did it. It was because of you. A way to be a part of your world, Ashley. The world you left me for."

It was Ashley's turn to shake her head. "But I thought that you didn't like Nashville. Didn't want me to go because it was a waste of time to try to make it in the music business. What I really thought you were saying was that I wasn't good enough."

Ty shook his head, his expression incredulous. "I don't know how you could have thought that. I never doubted that you would make it big. *Never*. And there was nothing I wanted more for you."

"But the night I told you about Rob's offer, you tried to talk me out of it."

Ty snorted. "Of course I did – you were leaving me. Running away with a blond pretty boy who promised to make your dreams come true. Sure, I had questions about the practical details – I am a businessman, after all – but that wasn't why I tried to stop you." He gave a small laugh, and looked down at his hands. "I was an ass that night, Ashley. A selfish, terrified, totally-in-love-with-you ass. I was worried about *you* and your future, but I should have started with the important part. I loved you, and didn't want to lose you."

Ty looked up, and Ashley gasped. His face was as open and raw as a wound, and love shone in his eyes. "I still feel that way, Ashley. I don't want to lose you again."

Tears welled up in her eyes, and she launched herself into Ty's lap. His hands came up to cradle her cheeks, and he poured all of his love into a kiss. When he pulled back his eyes were suspiciously bright.

"I love you, Ty," she said. I always have – and always will."

She glanced at Rob. He was staring at Ty with admiration on his face. Ty returned his look with a smile. Nothing had been said or openly resolved between those two, but they seemed at ease with one another once more, and that was good enough for now.

Rob cleared his throat. "So, we're all good here?" She and Ty nodded. Rob gave a bitter smile. "Then what do you say we see what our friend Brad wants?"

Ashley checked her phone. "I have three new texts, all telling me to call him or come by his office as soon as possible for good news."

Rob held up his phone. He'd received the texts too. "You want to call him or head over there?"

Ashley took a deep breath. "Let's go to his office. I want to see his face when he tries to explain what that whole solo thing was about. "

Rob nodded his agreement, and turned to Ty. "You're welcome to hang out here – we shouldn't be long."

Ty stood, shaking his head. "I need to run downtown. I was in such a rush to get here that I left my wallet in my office."

Ashley turned to him. "You have an office in Nashville?"

Ty looked sheepish. "That's where I slept last night."

That certainly explained why he looked so uncharacteristically rumpled this morning. She smiled. This new, casual Ty would take some getting used to.

Ashley got off Ty's lap, and he rose to his feet beside her. He wrapped a hand around the nape of her neck. "Good luck with Brad. Whatever he says or does, don't ever doubt that you have what it takes to make it. I support you every step of the way." He dropped a peck on her lips, then stepped back.

Rob was right behind him but instead of stepping out of the way, he let Ty bump right into him. Ty whirled so that the two men were practically nose-to-nose. They were of similar height, and looked each other in the eye.

Rob broke the silence first. "You'll be back later? So we

can... fill you in on what happens with Brad." The question seemed simple enough but there was nothing innocent about the heat in Rob's eyes.

Nor the answering flare of desire in Ty's. He cleared his throat. "Of course. I want to hear how things go with Brad – and what you want to do next."

Rob laughed, a sexy sound that resonated in Ashley's belly. "Oh, I have all kinds of things in mind." He leaned forward, and Ashley's heart raced. Was he going to kiss Ty? He raised a hand... and gave Ty an affectionate punch on the shoulder.

Ty smiled, and shoulder-bumped Rob as he headed for the door. They hadn't touched any more than two guys on a football field, but Ashley's blood was racing. Ty reached the door, but she was tempted to call him back. Forget the meeting with Brad – she wanted to get to the make-up sex.

She took a deep breath, and forced herself to focus. As much as she wanted to get naked with these two men again – and explore what that little display had been all about – there were things that needed to be done first.

Sweet Talk had a score to settle with Brad.

Chapter Twenty-Three

The receptionist announced Ashley and Rob's arrival through the intercom, then pointed them toward Brad's office. He stood as they entered, waving them into the big leather chairs that sat in front of his desk. "Rob. Ashley. Good to see you." He extended a hand across the desk, and Rob shook it, while Ashley sank into a chair. She crossed her arms, and sat back.

Brad was clearly pumped up with the news he had for them. He leaned forward. "I've got good news for you guys – big news."

Rob held up a hand, and looked over at Ashley. "Ashley and I want to talk to you first."

Brad looked between them, confusion on his face. His chair squeaked as he sat back. "Okay. What do you want to talk about?"

Ashley took a deep breath. "You proposed Rob as a solo act for opening night at the Roadhouse."

Surprise flashed across Brad's face, followed by guilt. Then his eyes narrowed. "Who told you that?"

Was he going to try to deny it?

Rob shrugged. "You're not the only one with connections in this town."

Ashley bit her lip – Ty would be amused to be called

connections.

Brad shrugged. "So I did – I told you I was going to start promoting you separately."

Rob surged forward. "You told me you were going to shift the pressure off Ashley, not break up Sweet Talk."

Brad raised his hands. "No one was breaking you up." He put mocking air quotes around the last words. "It was going to be one show. Anyway, the point is moot because they want both of you."

"No thanks to you," Ashley said. "We got that gig through our own connections."

A look of shock – *and was that fear?* – crossed Brad's face before he stifled it. He shook his head. "Look, I'm sorry if I went beyond what you were expecting." He looked at Ashley. "I never meant to cut you out or anything. If Rob did well, he would have been in a position to help you too."

Help her? Is that what Brad thought she needed? She opened her mouth to protest but he cut her off. "Anyway, that's all past – we should be focusing on the future. Sweet Talk's future."

Rob sat back. "Okay. Then talk to us about the future."

Brad steepled his fingers in the classic power position. It made Ashley's stomach turn.

He smiled "A scout from Atlas Studios was at your show last night, and they loved it. I'm going to talk to them today, and I'm pretty sure they're going to offer you a contract."

Atlas Studios? Contract? Butterflies started in Ashley's stomach, and her mouth went dry. She took a deep breath. "What kind of contract?"

"I don't know the details yet. I expect it will be the usual starting bid. They really like your first album, so they'll probably want more like that."

More like that. She looked over at Rob. He didn't say anything but Ashley knew what he was thinking. More of the same. More studio execs telling them what to play. More two-faced agents deciding what was best for them. Was that really what she wanted?

And what about Rob? There was no way he'd be content with the deal Atlas Studios was going to offer. Like Brad said, it would be more of the same. After three years together she and Rob were taking their personal relationship in a whole new direction. Why not do the same for their professional one too? Rob had had faith in her from the beginning, and all throughout her slump – wasn't it time she returned the favor by having some faith in his dreams?

Rob must have seen something in her eyes because his brows rose. Ashley gave a microscopic shake of her head. He continued to look confused for a moment, then his eyes widened, and he smiled.

Brad watched their exchange with an odd look. He'd obviously expected more enthusiasm. "Well? What do you think?"

Ashley kept her eyes on Rob as she answered. "I think that it's time for Sweet Talk to explore other opportunities, beyond those of the big studios. Independently."

Brad shook his head, clearly confused, but Rob knew exactly what she was saying. The happiness in his eyes brought tears to hers, and she had to swallow before she could continue. She turned back to Brad. "So tell Atlas Studios thanks, but no thanks."

Brad flopped back in his chair, his mouth open wide. It took a few attempts before he could speak. "What? Are you crazy?"

Rob leaned over, and kissed her on the mouth. Then he turned to Brad. "You heard her. We're done going the traditional route. We're heading out on our own."

Brad's mouth curved into a sneer. "An indie act? In Nashville? You think you can make it like that?"

Ashley shrugged. "Only one way to find out."

Brad crossed his arms. "You expect me to help you in this independent insanity? No way."

Ashley shrugged. "Then it's a good thing your contract is up soon. You're free to go your way, while we go ours."

Brad gave an incredulous snort. "After all the work I put in." He shook his head. "You'll regret this. An opportunity like this won't come around again."

Ashley nodded and stood. "You're right. We'll be making our own opportunities from now on. Good-bye, Brad." With that she turned on her heel, and marched out of the office. Rob was close behind. She held her breath, not wanting to spoil the drama of her exit with the hysterical laughter that was struggling in her chest.

She walked across the building's lobby, and stepped out into the sunlight. Rob was at her side. By unspoken agreement they said nothing as they stalked down the sidewalk. Rob led her to the car.

Ashley took a deep breath. "Holy shit, Rob – we just fired our manager."

He nodded.

The chirp of an incoming text sounded from Ashley's mobile phone, at the same time that Rob's phone beeped. "Ty," they said in unison. How strange and wonderful that they knew exactly who would be contacting both of them. And it seemed so natural.

Rather than dig through her purse Ashley let Rob read the text for both of them. He scanned the screen. "He's on his way back to the apartment, and wants to know what happened."

Ashley nodded, and Rob started typing a reply, speaking out loud as he did "We're on our way. Have interesting news."

He pressed send, and stuck the phone back into his pocket. "Wait 'til he hears that you fired Brad."

"What?" She pointed a finger at her chest. "*I* fired Brad?"

Rob leaned over, and kissed her. "You sure did, Ash. And it was a glorious thing, too."

They were walking up to the apartment building when Ty pulled up on his motorcycle. They stopped by the bike, and waited for him to dismount.

"You keep coming around like this," Rob said, slapping Ty on the shoulder, "we're gonna have to give you your own key."

Ty raised a brow, but she could see the idea pleased him. She smiled. It sounded like a good plan to her too.

She let them all into the apartment. The door hadn't even closed behind Ty before he asked, "What happened?"

Rob sprung the news. "So check it out – Ash fired Brad!"

She shook her head. "It wasn't just me—"

Rob sank into the couch, waving away her protest. "Don't listen to her – she was amazing. Told Brad what he could do with his studio contract."

Ty's eyes widened. "Studio contract? Brad had a contract for you, and you turned it down? Wasn't that what you wanted?"

Put like that, it did sound crazy, but Ashley couldn't regret her decision. "It wasn't the right thing for us. I didn't feel comfortable with the way Brad had been working behind our backs – even if he did have an explanation – and I realized that the traditional way wasn't going to work for us anymore. So I told him we weren't interested."

The admiration on Ty's face warmed her from the inside. Rob smiled, and clasped his hands together. "This calls for a celebration."

Ashley laughed. "We have no manager, no record deal. Great reasons to celebrate."

Rob's smile faded, and a look of concern settled on his face. "Ash? This is what you want too, isn't it? I mean I didn't force you into this decision, did I?"

She smiled, and waved his fear away. "I was just teasing you. It is a cause for celebration – because I have the perfect proposal for our future."

It had just come to her at that moment but it was so damned perfect she couldn't believe she hadn't thought of it sooner.

Both men turned to her. "You do?" Ty asked.

She nodded, cleared her throat, and spoke before she could lose her nerve. "You said you like challenges, right Ty?" She gestured at herself and Rob. "How about two of them?"

Rob's eyes went wide. "Ty can be our manager. Ash, that's freaking brilliant." He slapped Ty on the back. "What do you say?"

Ty looked floored. "You want me to manage Sweet Talk? But I know nothing about managing a band." He enunciated each word, as if to ensure that he was understanding them correctly and they, him.

Ashley spoke. "You don't know about negotiations? Contracts? Scheduling? That's most of what a manager does."

Ty paced away from the couch. He whirled back to them. "What about studio production, promotion, and all that?"

"You could learn that."

Ty looked skeptical, but Ashley could see the interest

brewing in his expression. "I don't know...," he said.

Rob braced his hands on his thighs. He looked at Ty with a wicked glint in his eye. "Don't think you can handle us both?"

Ashley's core muscles quivered at his tone. Ty's eyes went smoky, and his nostrils flared. "I could take you – no problem."

Rob stood up. He wiggled his fingers in a *bring-it-on* gesture.

Ty licked his lips, and gave Rob a look that made Ashley's inner muscles clench. *Hot damn.* Two hot guys in a crazy masculine display of power and sex appeal, and she had a ringside seat.

Ty stalked toward Rob until they were nose-to-nose again. Ty smiled that slow sexy smile that made her insides melt, cupped Rob's jaw in one hand, and brought his mouth down on Rob's.

Holy shit. It was hands down the hottest kiss Ashley had ever seen. Rob's hands came up to grab Ty's biceps, and pulled him closer. They were now chest-to-chest and rock hard, no doubt. She was getting wet just watching them.

A moment later they came up for breath, and Ty stepped back. His breathing was labored. "Well?"

Rob rubbed a hand over his mouth, and adjusted the front of his jeans. He swallowed. "You're hired."

Ty laughed. "Is that how you interviewed Brad too?"

"I bet Brad would have loved that," Ashley said. "I think he was secretly hot for Rob. Well, he could have been," she added when Rob rolled his eyes.

Rob shuddered. "That weasel – I wouldn't touch him with a ten-foot pole."

Ty looked down at Rob's crotch. "Dude, I know you're packing some serious meat down there, but ten feet?"

Rob rubbed his hand over the bulge that swelled behind his fly. "I don't know exactly how big it is but I can tell you it's growing by the minute."

Their banter was corny but Ashley's response came out more like a moan than a groan. Rob looked at her, then looked at Ty. "What do you say we seal the deal?" Ty smiled his agreement. "An excellent idea." Rob and Ty turned towards her, hunger in their eyes.

Ashley's mouth went dry. They stalked toward her, and her heart raced. Her breasts swelled. These men – *both* of these men – wanted her. Loved her. Needed her the way she needed them. Now and forever. Warmth filled her chest as heat flooded between her thighs.

Rob reached a hand to her. With trembling fingers, she placed her palm in his. She rose, and Ty wrapped an arm around her waist, leaning in to nuzzle her throat. Rob buried a hand in her hair, and tugged her forward for a kiss that left her heart pounding. The men led her down the hall, divesting her of clothing with every kiss and caress. By the time they reached Rob's room, she was wearing only panties and her bra but they were still dressed. Not fair.

She took a step away from Ty, and slipped out from under Rob's arm. She planted her hands on her hips. "Take your clothes off – both of you."

Rob's eyes flared. "Nothing hotter than a girl who knows what she wants." Ty nodded. They tugged off their clothes with haste, until two naked men stood before her. Two sets of washboard abs. Two solid muscled chests. Two strong proud cocks.

Ashley knelt on the bed so that she was eye-level with all that long, hard goodness. She reached forward, and grasped one in each hand, pulling gently. With twin groans, the men responded, following her tugs until they were facing one another, each with a knee braced on the bed. Now that was power.

She stared at the bounty in her hands, and licked her lips. Two cocks right in front of her, jutting towards one another. Another step closer, and the men would embrace. The thought of them pleasuring each other made her so hot. For now, she'd focus on pleasuring them. At the same time. She glanced up. Both men watched her with half-lidded eyes. Damn this was fun. A drop of pre-cum appeared on the tip of Rob's cock. She licked it off, then traced the narrow slit on top with her tongue. Rob shuddered, and she heard Ty groan. She smiled. Would Rob groan if she licked Ty?

She flicked her tongue over the head of Ty's cock, looking up as she did. His eyes burned with heat, his jaw clenched. She took the head fully into her mouth, gently running her tongue along the underside. Then she sucked hard. Ty growled, and his hips twitched forward, but he remained in control. She'd have to do something about that.

She turned to Rob, and gave his erection the same treatment. Then back to Ty. She alternated between them, licking, sucking, playing. Nipping the smooth skin where their cocks met their bodies. Taking their balls in her hands, and kneading them. The men groaned, and gripped her shoulders. Subtle tremors rocked their bodies.

Time to turn it up a notch. She turned to Rob, and without warning, took his cock into her mouth, as deep as it would go. He gasped. Her other hand gripped Ty's cock, and she pumped, slowly then gaining speed and strength. From tip to base and back, she stroked them, one with her mouth, the other with her hand. Then she switched. Now she sucked Ty's cock, her mouth going up and down his length, while her fist pumped Rob's. From one hot cock to the other, she went back and forth. Tasting them, feeling them until she couldn't tell one from the other. Couldn't recall who stood where.

When both men were groaning, and squirming she stopped. Tugging again she pulled them forward until the tips were nearly touching – and then they *were* touching. They got what she was trying to do, and moved closer – now their cocks were pushed together. A delicious double-scoop all for her.

She brushed her lips over them, bumping over one purple head, then the other. Licked across them. Her tongue swirled around, and in-between. Shudders traveled though the men's bodies, and into the hard cocks she held in her hands. That she could have two such strong men at her mercy. Make them feel such pleasure. Lust roared through her body.

With one last suck at each head she released their cocks, then leaned back onto her hands. She still wore her bra and panties. She reached around behind her back and unsnapped her bra, then slipped it slowly down her arms. She lay back on the bed, looped two fingers under the narrow waistband of her panties, and slid them down her thighs. Ty pounced, reaching for her before she even got the material to her knees. Rob grabbed the fabric, wrenched it off, and tossed it to the side.

Ty lay beside her, and kissed her while Rob parted her thighs. Like the first time, Ty's tongue invaded her mouth while Rob's laved her clit. She writhed under the combined assault. Her pleasure built quickly, until she was on the edge of an orgasm. Rob must have sensed it because he gave her a long slow suck, then pulled back. She moaned but was grateful. She wanted this, their first time together as a trio, to last.

Rob crawled up her body, bracketing her head with his

arms. He gave her a long hard kiss, then pressed his hips against hers. Yeah, that felt good – no, it felt great – but she wanted something different this time. Something special. With a playful smile she bucked with her hips, and pressed up on his shoulders. He got the message, and rolled onto his back.

Ashley straddled Rob. She looked over to make sure Ty was watching, then she got up on her knees, and positioned her pussy over Rob's cock. She slowly lowered herself, and Rob pressed upwards, filling her completely. At this angle she could feel his cock reaching up into her womb, rubbing every sensitive nerve.

She turned to Ty for a kiss, but he had moved behind her. She looked over her shoulder wondering what he was doing – and saw him sitting back on his heels, his hand was fisted around his cock. His gaze was fixed on the point where Rob's cock disappeared into her slit. She leaned forward, letting her chest rest against Rob's, and arched her back to give Ty a better view.

"See anything you like?" She said. Ty's answering chuckle came out as a groan.

Rob reached behind her, and gripped her butt cheeks in his hands. He squeezed lightly, then pulled them gently apart, opening her further to Ty's view. The position stretched her anus, and pleasure shot through her.

She heard the sound of sucking behind her and then a moist finger ringed her sensitive pucker. She groaned, and it slipped inside. Oh Lord, she had Rob's cock in her pussy and Ty's finger in her ass. Damn it felt good.

"Think you can handle us both, Ash?" Rob asked softly. She looked at him with a puzzled expression. Then looked at Ty. His eyes were wide, his cock twitched. He seemed to understand what Rob was talking about.

Did he mean…? She gasped. Two men, two cocks inside her at once. It scared her a bit, but at the same time she wanted to know what it would feel like. She nodded.

"Are you sure?" Ty asked. She turned to him, and nodded more vigorously. "We'll go slow," he said.

"Ok. Yes. Sounds good," she said. She could hear the eagerness in her voice.

"I don't think she's worried," Rob said with a laugh, and nodded towards the bedside table. "There's lube and condoms in there, Ty."

Ty retrieved the lube and a condom then climbed back onto the bed. Ashley leaned even farther forward until her chest was pressed against Rob's. She felt Ty shift on the mattress, and heard the squirt of the lube. Then the pressure of his fingers. He pressed one inside, then another. He paused. He'd obviously done this before. She relaxed, and let his fingers go deeper, and slide out. In then out again. Rob stayed still within her slit, and she flexed her inner muscles around him in time with Ty's movements.

After a few more thrusts, Ty's hand stilled and pulled away from her. He shifted behind her, and put his hands on her ass. The tip of his cock touched her from behind

She froze. Both Ty and Rob were big. Would they fit? Could she take them both?

"It's ok, Ash," Rob said, stroking a hand over her hair. "We don't have to do this."

She looked into his beautiful brown eyes, then over her shoulder at Ty's blue ones. It had been so good when Rob had filled her back there. It felt so good to have him inside her now.

Yes, she wanted this. Wanted to take both of her lovers into her body at the same time.

Ty spoke. "If you don't want to do this say so, and we'll stop."

"No," she said. He moved away, and she groaned with disappointment. "I mean no, don't stop."

Ty laughed. "I like a woman who knows what she wants."

"I know exactly what I want – to feel both of your cocks inside me at the same time." She dropped her voice to a growl. "And I want it now."

Rob's cock twitched within her, and Ty moaned. "Your wish is my command, Ashley."

Ty kneeled behind her. Once again she felt his cock at her back entrance. Rob pulled back until he was almost out, and Ty pushed forward. There was a stinging sensation but it felt good too. Still, her body clenched by instinct.

Rob whispered in her ear. "Relax. Remember how good it felt with me? This will be even better."

"I'm trying," she replied.

He chuckled. "Let me help."

Rob stretched up, and took her nipple in his mouth, sucking and licking. She relaxed but only a little – it was hard to let go completely even though she knew she wanted this. That it would feel good. Then Rob nipped, sending a shot of pleasure from nipple to clit – Her muscles trembled, and Ty gained another inch.

"Damn," Ty whispered, and she nodded. Damn was right. She angled her hips, trying to let him in. He paused until she looked back. "You want more Ashley? You sure?"

"Yes, I'm sure."

Without warning, Ty slapped her butt cheek. As she was reeling from the shock – and the incredible pleasure-pain it gave her – he pushed forward in one quick smooth thrust. His balls pressed against her slit from behind. She trembled with pleasure.

"You okay?" he asked as if between clenched teeth.

She moaned. "Oh God, yes. That feels amazing."

"My turn," Rob said. He flexed his hips slowly and entered her. "Damn that feels tight. And so fucking good."

Ashley could only moan her agreement. When Rob was fully seated, Ty pulled back again. He groaned. "Damn. I can feel..."

She smiled. "Rob's cock inside me?"

Ty's voice was rough. "Every inch."

Rob retreated, and Ty advanced. Ty pulled back, and Rob pressed forward. The men found a rhythm between them – sometimes both inside her body, sometimes alternating. Ashley could only hold still and let them move, her limbs quivering with intense pleasure. The ecstasy built to thunderous climax that crashed over her like a tsunami. Her body jerked, and quivered like a marionette on a string. Her mind went blank, short-circuited by the pleasure that lit her ever nerve.

She collapsed onto Rob, her limbs sprawling around him.

Both men stopped, waiting, their breath coming hard. She could tell they were close. She could let them continue, and find their pleasure in her body, but she had another idea. "I'm done," she said, and wriggled her hips.

They got the idea, and each pulled back. The emptiness felt strange after being so full.

Rob pulled her onto his chest. His still-hard cock pressed into her belly but he held her tenderly. She felt Ty rub her butt cheek where he'd slapped – *spanked* – her, and his lips kissed her gently on the spot.

She smiled. After a moment she pulled away from Rob, and flopped onto her back. Ty sat back on his heels, and pulled the condom off his still hard cock. Rob put his hands behind his head, and looked to her. Both seemed to be waiting for her to say what to do next. And she knew exactly what she wanted to see – something she'd fantasized about since she first spotted Ty's motorcycle on Music Row. "I want to see the two of you together."

Ty coughed in surprise. Rob's eyes darkened with lust. "Like in your fantasy Ash?"

She nodded.

Ty looked between them. "Fantasy?"

Ashley felt her face heat – which was ridiculous considering what they'd been doing. Rob nodded. "Last week she admitted to fantasizing about me. With other men."

Had that only been last week? Damn a lot had changed since then. "Actually Rob, when you came in the other night, after we saw Ty's motorcycle, I was imagining you with him."

Now Rob was speechless, but Ty smiled "As your new manager, it's my job to make your Nashville dreams come true."

"Hot damn," Rob whispered. He rolled onto his belly, got up on his knees, and looked back at Ty. "You ready for this?" There was no challenge in his voice, just a gentle question.

Ty's lips curved in a slow smile. "I told you already – I can take you."

Rob's eyes narrowed. He reached over his shoulder, and waggled his fingers as he had before. "Then bring it on, man. Bring. It. On."

Ty scooted forward, and placed his hands on Rob, rubbing them over his back and ass. Rob arched into the touch, nodding his chin towards the bedside table. Ashley retrieved another condom. She dug in the sheets until she found the lube. She crawled over to Ty, but pulled back when he reached for them. "Allow me."

Ashley rolled the condom down Ty's cock. Then she squirted some lube on her fingers and turned to Rob. She circled his anus with her fingers until he growled, then scooted back. She leaned back against the pillows, and settled in to watch her wildest fantasy unfold.

Ty gripped Rob's ass, and brought his cock to the other man's opening. Rob braced himself, and nodded, then Ty started to push in. Ty went faster than he had with Ashley but clearly too slow for Rob's taste.

Rob glanced over his shoulder, his eyes narrowed. "That the best you can do?" He shook his head in disappointment but Ashley could hear the playfulness in his voice. "I'm a man, Ty. I'm not going to break."

Ty's nostrils flared, and he flexed his hips. Then he buried himself in Rob's ass so hard they both slid forward on the bed.

Rob cried out. "Fuck, that feels good."

Ty nodded and pulled back, thrusting hard again and again. There was nothing slow or gentle between these two, not the way they had been with Ashley. These were two men pushing each other. Testing each other. Finding pleasure in the rough way that men can only do together.

It was so much sexier than Ashley had imagined. With every thrust of Ty's cock, Ashley's nipples tingled. Every moan from Rob's lips made her clit spark. Soon she was squirming and wet. She thought about the vibrator in her bedside drawer but didn't want to leave the room and miss a moment. Instead she spread her legs, and brought her fingers to her clit, her eyes fixed on the men.

Rob's eyes were closed tightly. She called his name, and he looked up. Then his gaze dropped down to where her fingers played over her clit. He'd wanted to watch her pleasure herself – she was happy to oblige.

"Damn, Ash. That's hot," he said, gasping as Ty slammed him harder than before. Ty looked up and groaned as well. She spread her legs wider to give them a better view, and brought her other hand to her slit. She slipped a finger inside, fucking herself with her hand while Ty fucked Rob in the ass.

"Ty," Rob said, and the other man stilled. Rob nodded his head towards her open legs, and pulled forward. Ty followed so they were still joined. Rob's head hovered over her slit. Ty resumed his thrusts, faster than before, and Rob leaned down. She kept rubbing her clit, but Rob's tongue replaced the fingers in her slit, thrusting in time with the pumps of Ty's cock in his ass.

Her gaze went to Ty's. His eyes glowed with love, so strong it was like a touch. Her body shuddered, her pleasure catching her unaware. She arched into Rob's mouth, crying out. He kept licking and sucking until pleasure took him too. He pushed back, pressing against Ty. His cock jerked, spilling seed onto his covers. Ty kept pumping, his eyes on Ashley, until he too was driven over the edge. Ty pressed into Rob, and threw his head back with a cry.

Both men panted for a moment, chests heaving in sync. Then Ty pulled back. Rob tugged the damp covers off the bed and they all crawled under the sheets for a long, soft cuddle. Ashley was snuggled between the men, but their fingers entwined over her head.

She looked at the clock. It was mid-afternoon, and she was hungry, but too tired to go anywhere. Too happy and relaxed to move. She tried to push the thought of food away but her tummy growled.

"I think our girl needs some food." Ty said.

Rob got up. "I'm on it." He slipped out of the bedroom.

The two men took turns feeding her in bed. She felt like an ancient queen – a goddess – being attended to by her harem. She chuckled at the thought of Rob and Ty dressed in silk pantaloons. No, if they were her harem she'd keep them naked all the time.

"What are you chuckling about?" Rob asked.

She waved her hand, her mouth too full to explain. "My harem. No pantaloons. Naked."

Rob made a sound of mock outrage. "Are you saying we're your harem?"

Ty laughed. "I think she's saying that if we were her harem she wouldn't dress us in pantaloons, but have us go naked all the time."

She pointed at Ty as if to say "got it" and both men laughed.

Rob turned to Ty. "Now you've done it. You said her wish was your command, and it's gone to her head."

Ty smiled. "Well if she's looking for a love slave, I'm happy to apply for the job."

"Then I guess I'll have to become one too," Rob said. "She can't have a harem with only one man."

Ashley laughed, her heart full of love for the two men in her bed. In her life. Now and forever. A perfect Nashville Trio.

Acknowledgements

For Louise Fury, my dear friend, and the best and smartest agent in the world for encouraging me since the day we met, and guiding me through the crazy-fun world of publishing. To my beta readers, especially Carole-Ann Warburton, for critiquing and loving early versions of this manuscript. Coat of Polish Editing, for helping me make this story and its characters as strong and compelling as they could be. Randall Luttenberg, for the wonderful design talent and patience that went into my super-hot cover. Paige Price of Electra Edits, for catching every misplaced or missing comma and assuring me that my Southern wasn't half-bad. Tahra Seplowin, for her formatting talents, and many years of support and encouragement. Cherra of I Love Bookie Nookie Reviews, for all of her Goodreads support, and a fabulous cover reveal. Louisa Bacio, blurb-genius for helping me entice, not bore, potential readers. Denny S. Bryce for all of her plotting help, including the suggestion of the essential Basketball Scene. Michele Monkou, for reading multiple copies and pieces of this manuscript, and giving on-target feedback every time. My children, for encouraging "Mommy's writing", and not killing each other or burning down the house while I was distracted with this story, and of course, my favorite romance hero, my husband Physics Guys, for believing in me, and this crazy dream of writing, before I did. I love you.

About the Author

Joy Daniels writes romance that's Smart, Sexy and Down-to-Earth. She loves erotic romance because it allows her to expose her characters completely – strengths, flaws and scars. She's originally from New York City, (and still a loyal Yankees fan!), but since moving south, she's developed passions for NASCAR and country music. Both feature in her recent stories. In addition to writing (and reading!) she enjoys yoga, bellydancing, and growing veggies in the Washington, D.C. area with her scientist husband and two curious kids. She loves to hear from readers so drop her a note at authorjoydaniels@gmail.com, stop by www.authorjoydaniels, or find her on Facebook at https://www.facebook.com/joy.daniels.author.

Enjoyed Nashville Trio?
Check out...

Revving Her Up
Full Throttle, Book 1
Joy Daniels

Her love life is running on empty. And he's just the man to make her engine purr.

Sarah Lange's career as a New York lawyer is in high gear—and the stress has left her hormones sputtering. With strict doctor's orders to relax, she books the cure: a spa vacation in the cool, green mountains of Virginia.

When a pothole sends her Porsche to the side of the road, she finds herself stuck in small-town Rapture. She'd love nothing more than to blow this Hicksville and be on her way...until she meets sexy stockcar mechanic Cole Cassidy .

Coles knows exactly how to handle that fancy car, and its uptight driver. Sarah's not his type, but neither can deny that their attraction is firing on all cylinders. Soon he's introducing her to the thrill of speed at the local track—in his car, and on it.

But Sarah's troubles aren't so easily left in the dust. Unless she forces herself to decide if she's willing and able to let someone else take the wheel.

Warning: Contains a false start, breakdowns of the automotive and erotic kinds, creative uses of shower massagers and silk ties, and thrill-rides in, on, and outside of a racecar.

Chapter One

Sarah Lange slid out of the low bucket seat of her Porsche convertible. Heart pounding, she rounded the vehicle's front end and froze. Now she knew why the car had skidded out of that damned pothole, listing heavily to the right—the right front wheel stuck out at a forty-five degree angle. It reminded her of the tooth she'd knocked askew falling off her bike in the fourth grade. Somehow she suspected the repair would be even more painful.

This was so not what she needed right now. She resisted the urge to kick the bent wheel and retrieved her bag and phone from the car. The reception sucked, but she managed to get through to the roadside assistance center. After describing the damage as best she could, she sent them her coordinates. If this road had a name, it hadn't shown up on her GPS.

Tendrils of hair stuck to her forehead. The short wool trench coat that had been perfect for a January day in Manhattan felt like a wraparound sauna here in Virginia. A trickle of sweat inched its way down her back as her shoulders crept up toward her ears. Relax. She removed the coat and slipped it into the car, then forced herself to take a deep breath. The scent of fresh-cut grass and cow manure filled her nostrils. Hardly the aromatherapy she'd been looking forward to. She wrinkled her nose and took another breath, a bit shallower this time. Relax.

An hour passed. Where the hell was her tow?

She was dialing for the third time when a lone chipmunk crept out of the grass a few yards away. It approached the road, pausing at the edge of the asphalt to sniff the air.

"You can cross. I haven't seen a car since I got off the highway." The creature's head swiveled to face her, its tiny body poised for flight. She lowered her voice. "Go on, little guy. There's no need for both of us to be stuck here." The chipmunk tilted his head, as if assessing the truth of her words, then trotted out onto the asphalt. The air stirred as Sarah watched it disappear into the trees. A dull roar signaled the approach of another vehicle. Finally.

Sarah pushed away from where she'd been leaning against the car and looked down the road. She watched a blue pickup truck come to a stop on the opposite shoulder. The driver's door opened and a man in a cowboy hat stepped out. He was tall and broad-shouldered in a way that she found immediately reassuring.

The man crossed the road with long, relaxed strides. He wore a plaid shirt over a white tee, faded jeans and worn work boots. His height forced Sarah to tilt her head back to focus on his face as he got closer. Most of it was cast into shadow by his black cowboy hat, emphasizing the strength of his jaw and the dark scruff that covered it. Even without seeing his face Sarah could tell he was attractive, if one was into big and brawny. Which she wasn't.

Her body had reached a different conclusion. A shiver raced down her spine as the deep muscles below her navel tightened and goose bumps rose on her arms—the physical equivalent of oooh, big, strong man! She squared her shoulders, ignoring her primitive damsel-in-distress reaction. She needed someone to help her with her car and presumably he could. Weren't guys in small towns always working on cars?

There couldn't be much else to do.

Cole Cassidy hadn't expected an eclipse today, but he couldn't deny what he'd seen—one heavenly body passing before another. What else would he call a sexy blonde crossing in front of a Porsche convertible? Other than his lucky day.

The woman and her car were not as lucky. Even at a distance he'd seen the vehicle leaning to the right. He couldn't tell why—he had a hard time taking his eyes off the woman standing next to it. Her hands were on her hips, a pose that stretched her black V-neck across her high, round breasts. She wore a slim black skirt and high-heeled leather boots. Sleek sunglasses hid her eyes. He didn't need the New York plates to tell him she wasn't from around here.

"Afternoon, ma'am." He tipped his hat. "Car trouble?"

"That's an understatement," she said with a growl, dropping a cell phone into the expensive-looking purse hanging over her shoulder.

"You call for a tow?"

"Yes, but who knows how long that will take? It's already been an hour."

Given how few calls they got out here, Cole suspected it wouldn't be much longer, but he didn't want to make any promises. "Lemme see."

He dropped into a crouch to look beneath the car. Leaning the way it was, the sports car was too low to see under. With the woman standing over him, he had no trouble checking out the spiky heels of her boots or the smooth black leather that hugged her legs up to the knees.

He stood. "Can't see much from here. What happened?"

She huffed, making her blond bangs dance. "There's a damned crater in the road back there. It's right after the bend so I couldn't see it until I was in it."

He nodded in sympathy. "That'd do it."

The blonde took a deep breath, her tension palpable. He

resisted the urge to put a soothing hand on her arm. She didn't seem like the type who'd appreciate the gesture. She opened her mouth to say something but was interrupted by the arrival of the tow truck from over the rise. It passed them and pulled onto the shoulder in a spray of gravel.

Cole raised a hand in greeting as a big man in an oil-stained T-shirt and John Deere ball cap got out of the truck. "Hey, Mike."

"Cole. Whatcha doing here, man?"

"Came upon this nice lady stranded by the side of the road and stopped to see if I could help."

The driver turned to the "nice lady" and Cole could see his eyes widen. They didn't get women like her around here. "Ma'am," Mike said, touching a hand to the brim of his cap.

She nodded, her lips tight.

He turned back to Cole. "Surprised to see you here. Austin heard you'd be out of town for a bit."

Cole nodded. "I was just on my way back."

"From Mooresville, right? I bet it was exciting, with everyone getting ready—"

The blonde stepped between them, annoyance clear on her face. "Excuse me," she said, her tone anything but polite. "I'm in a bit of a hurry. So if you could save the catching up for later..." She waved at the car. Cole bit back a smile.

Mike's face reddened. "Of course. What's the problem?"

Before she could launch into an explanation, Cole spoke up. "If you've got it under control, Mike, I'm gonna take off."

The woman glanced at him, surprise and something else flashing across her face. Disappointment? It was gone too quickly for Cole to be sure.

"Okay," Mike said. "Be seeing you later, eh?"

Cole looked over at the blonde. Her arms were crossed, the

toe of one leather boot tapping impatiently. Her attitude sent up all sorts of red flags but his body didn't care. His cock stirred behind his fly.

"Oh, you can bet on it."

Available at all major eRetailers.

Turn the page for another excerpt...

Hide and Seek
Joy Daniels

A Family Mystery...

All her life, shy history buff Evie Ryder has heard whispers of scandal about her namesake great aunt. When she's invited to a party in Aunt Evangeline's haunted mansion, Evie can't resist the opportunity to investigate the woman's secrets.

A Sexy Surprise – or Two...

At the party, Evie makes a different kind of discovery – among the guests are two men she shared passionate kisses with under the mistletoe. Sophisticated former model Sebastian Duval arouses her deepest desires, while the clever hands of sexy chef Drew Collins make her crave his touch. Refusing to come between the best friends, Evie backs off. But Sebastian and Drew have a different idea.

A Passionate Legacy...

Guided by an unseen presence, Evie discovers the truth about her aunt's life, and embraces the pleasure of her own erotic inheritance.

From Hide and Seek...

I slipped into the house through the back door and was heading for the hall when the doorbell rang. Suzie arrived at the door at the same time as the butler and stepped aside to let the Mason pull the door open.

I leaned to the side to catch a glimpse of the newest arrival and sucked in a breath.

A tall dark-skinned man stood in the doorway. He had dark eyes that slanted over high cheekbones, and a full arrogant mouth made for sin. The afternoon sun caressed him with warm light highlighting the width of his shoulders and the natural grace of his posture. He had a long black leather coat and a travel bag slung over his arm.

"Sebastian! I'm so glad you could make it." Suzie threw her arms around the man's neck and his arms came around her waist. The memory of those arms around me – and the kiss that had followed – made my mouth go dry.

As if I'd broadcast my thoughts, Sebastian's gaze swept past Suzie to land on me. He scanned me from head to toe, and my nipples tightened as if he'd caressed me with his hands. Flustered, I wrapped my arms around my waist.

Suzie stepped back and turned to follow Sebastian's gaze. She beckoned me forward with a wave.

"Evie, come meet Sebastian, one of Blake's oldest friends from childhood. Sebastian, this is my cousin and roommate, Evie. We share the great-great aunt who owned this house."

He held out a hand. "Evie." His smooth British accent sent liquid heat into my belly.

I placed my palm to his and a jolt of awareness shot up my arm and down my torso to lodge deep in my belly. I dropped his hand in shock. He must have noticed my reaction because the corner of his mouth shifted up a fraction of an inch.

Suzie looked from Sebastian to me and back again, a curious frown on her face. "Have you two already met?"

My head was frozen but Sebastian gave a slow nod. "We met at your holiday party." Had I imagined a slight emphasis on the word met? My face heated.

Suzie seemed oblivious to my discomfort. She turned to address the butler. "Mason, please bring Mr. Duval's things to the Oak Room in the East Corridor." Mason nodded and reached for Sebastian's bag. Sebastian slid it off his shoulder and handed it to the man with the casual manner of someone used to servants. From his poise and wardrobe, I wasn't surprised.

Suzie turned back to Sebastian. His gaze remained on me just a moment too long, and I could feel my body react to his attention.

Suzie spoke to both of us. "The other guests will be arriving throughout the afternoon. Feel free to explore the house, and if you're hungry, there are meat pasties cooling in the kitchen. Dinner will be at seven."

So my appropriation of the pastie hadn't been theft after all. Maybe I would grab another.

"Will we be dressing for dinner this evening?"

Dressing for dinner? He asked as if it were a normal thing.

Suzie shook her head. "No. That's one aspect of house parties I always hated, so we'll be casual at meals."

Sebastian nodded. "Then I will find my room and unpack." He turned to me. "I look forward to catching up with you later."

Catching up? Other than some whispered flirting and that amazing kiss we didn't know each other at all. But with Suzie's curious gaze on me, I plastered on a smile and nodded.

Sebastian strode passed us and started up the stairs. It took all my willpower not to turn and watch him ascend. Suzie had no such compunction and whirled around.

She sighed. "He is beautiful."

I looked at her in surprise. "Suzie, you're engaged."

"Of course I am, but I'm not blind." She gestured to the

landing where Sebastian was turning the corner. "I heard that Sebastian modeled a bit while he was in university and it's clear he hasn't forgotten how to move." She shook her head. "Damn."

Well, now I had to watch. Just my luck, Sebastian reached the top at that precise moment, turned and caught us ogling him.

I blushed and looked away but Suzie waved. "Just enjoying the view!"

Sebastian's laugh was a deep, sexy sound and I looked up to see him taking a bow. He disappeared into the corridor and I grabbed Suzie's arm. "I thought you said Blake's friends weren't coming from the UK?"

"They aren't." She pulled her arm away and looked at me as if I were acting strange. "Sebastian got a commission in New York so he moved here a couple of months ago. Took an apartment in our neighborhood with Drew, another friend of Blake's." She narrowed her eyes. "You wouldn't happen to have run into him at our party, too?"

I shook my head. What was the likelihood that Drew was the other man whom I'd kissed that night?

Available at all major eRetailers.

www.ingramcontent.com/pod-product-compliance
Lightning Source LLC
Chambersburg PA
CBHW022014170626
46808CB00001B/410